Dying for Murder

A Cordi O'Callaghan Mystery

DYING
for murder

Suzanne F. Kingsmill

DUNDURN
TORONTO

Editor: Cheryl Hawley
Design: Courtney Horner
Printer: Webcom

Library and Archives Canada Cataloguing in Publication

Kingsmill, Suzanne, author
        Dying for murder / by Suzanne F. Kingsmill.
(A Cordi O'Callaghan mystery ; 3)
Issued in print and electronic formats.
ISBN 978-1-4597-0818-1

        I. Title.

PS8621.I57D95 2013   C813'.6   C2013-905475-8
                                                        C2013-905476-6

1   2   3   4   5   18   17   16   15   14

Conseil des Arts
du Canada   Canada Council
for the Arts   Canada   ONTARIO ARTS COUNCIL
CONSEIL DES ARTS DE L'ONTARIO

We acknowledge the support of the **Canada Council for the Arts** and the **Ontario Arts Council** for our publishing program. We also acknowledge the financial support of the **Government of Canada** through the **Canada Book Fund** and **Livres Canada Books**, and the **Government of Ontario** through the **Ontario Book Publishing Tax Credit** and the **Ontario Media Development Corporation**.

Care has been taken to trace the ownership of copyright material used in this book. The author and the publisher welcome any information enabling them to rectify any references or credits in subsequent editions.

J. Kirk Howard, President

The publisher is not responsible for websites or their content unless they are owned by the publisher.

Printed and bound in Canada.

Visit us at
Dundurn.com | @dundurnpress | Facebook.com/dundurnpress | Pinterest.com/dundurnpress

Dundurn
3 Church Street, Suite 500
Toronto, Ontario, Canada
M5E 1M2

Gazelle Book Services Limited
White Cross Mills
High Town, Lancaster, England
LA1 4XS

Dundurn
2250 Military Road
Tonawanda, NY
U.S.A. 14150

Hey, Tim and Jesse!
Mother and sons forever!

chapter one

There was someone in my car. There shouldn't have been. It was 4:30 and most of the cars in the parking lot at the zoology building at Sussex University, where I work as an assistant professor, were gone for the day. I cautiously approached, then stopped dead as the rear lights flashed on and off and I heard the engine cough to life. *Must be a friend*, I thought, and immediately knew I was being ridiculous or deliberately blind. What friend borrows a car without asking and without keys? I stood glued to the spot as the car backed out. It was a man, but I couldn't see his face easily because he was on the other side of the car and my eyesight stinks. All I could see was his profile. My brain finally alerted my body that something was amiss and that perhaps I should do something about it. There was also a distant rumbling that maybe I shouldn't, maybe he had a gun or a knife or a can of mace, even a taser. But it was only a distant rumbling and I launched myself at the car, pounding on the passenger window. That got him turning. I could see he was wearing a deep-maroon hoodie; faded, ripped jeans; and a crooked smile, which he flashed at me as he gave me the finger and stepped on the gas. That did it. I was damned if I was going to let him get away. I started sprinting after him as he turned down onto the main street close to the university. I could see the traffic building and knew I had a chance. Of course, what I'd do when I got to him I wasn't quite sure, but I sprinted down the road after him anyway. I saw his taillights go red and sped up. I was thirty feet and closing when he suddenly swung right down a back lane. I couldn't lose him, not with the valuable cargo in my car.

When I reached the lane I skidded to a stop and eyeballed the situation. It was one of those lanes that divide the backsides of one row of houses from the other. My car was about fifteen feet away, its brake lights were on, and a massive moving van was blocking its way. I had him. I could see him looking back at me through my rear windshield, and this time I smiled. He responded by jerking my gears into reverse and stepping on the gas. I hadn't been ready for that and the car barrelled down on me. I moved then, but not quite fast enough. The car brushed me and knocked me off my feet. With my face in the dirt, I turned and watched as my car careened down the lane, came to a screeching halt, ground the gears back into forward, and disappeared down an off-shoot of the lane I was lying in. I got to my feet, feeling impotent and angry, and gingerly loped over to the fork in the road. My car was already at the end of it, pushing its way into traffic by sitting on its horn. My horn. My car. It occurred to me briefly that maybe my car and what was in it weren't worth it, but it was my car and he was stealing it. So I loped down the lane, my right side aching from the fall. When I reached the main street my hopes rose; there was lots of traffic. I scanned the cars ahead of me and there it was: my little Mini moving at about my speed. I ran faster, my heart catching up, until I was right behind him.

Then he made his move. He floored it, jumped the curb, and raced along the sidewalk, pedestrians scattering like so many leaves in the wind as my car gained speed at an alarming rate. I guess he wasn't a very good driver, or maybe he was actually scared of me because he swerved to miss a fire hydrant, lost control, and slalomed through the linen-covered outdoor tables of a little cafe. I saw the driver bail out just before the car took a one-way ticket to the recycling depot. The sound of crunching metal, breaking glass, and screaming people was overwhelmed by the horrendous crash of the car into the solid brick wall of the little restaurant. I stood transfixed, watching the car crumple into uselessness. I could see my thief running away from all the commotion. I almost ran after him but I was caught in a surreal moment as I watched my faithful little car burst into flames. It wasn't so much the car that kept me standing there in disbelief. It was what had been in it. But I couldn't dwell upon that now. It would have to wait.

The police were very efficient and took my statement in record time. They assured me they would be in touch as the case proceeded. I wondered how long I would have been tied up with them if someone had died. It had taken a lot longer to get to a rental agency and organize a car, and I'd had to settle for an old vermilion clunker from the guys who rent wrecks. Traffic was pretty bad on the Champlain Bridge, but I still made it home in record time. It always feels wonderfully therapeutic when I turn off the main highway and down the lane where I live in an old log cabin on a five-hundred-acre dairy farm I share with my brother, Ryan, and his wife and kids.

I was alarmed when I saw two cars in my driveway and then mystified to see two people on my porch. And then I remembered that I'd invited my lab tech Martha Bathgate and her boyfriend, my pathologist friend Duncan Macpherson, for dinner. Martha was staring at me with her mouth open as I got out of the car, her face signalling, as it always does, what she was thinking. But I wasn't sure what that was — shock at the colour of my new car or panic because she had looked in my fridge, which she always did, and seen nothing and now here I was empty handed with dinner on the horizon. Martha loved her food, her sturdy rotund frame caressing every pound like a long-lost friend. I looked at them looking at me, arms empty, and blurted out, "Someone tried to steal my car."

They both started talking at once but Duncan's deep baritone won out. "Spill it," he said with a smile that almost took my eyes off his nose. Almost. I just couldn't get over that nose. It was so present. Big and bulbous it dwarfed the rest of his face. I shuddered to think what it must have been like as a teenager to get a zit on that nose. But then again, it was so big that a zit wouldn't have made much difference.

I pulled myself together and spilled it. When I was finished there was dead silence.

"Jesus, Cordi. That's pretty stupid," Martha, who hardly ever minced her words, eventually said. She was sitting in the hammock, putting a severe dent in it. Her curly black hair framed the tiny, perfect features of her round face like a sunflower. "I mean, why would you chase him like that? No car is worth the risk."

"It wasn't the car," I said. "It was what was in the car."

"Which was?" asked Duncan, whose stomach had started to growl. *What was I going to feed them?* I wondered.

"The recordings of Indigo Bunting songs that I just brought back from Point Pelee yesterday." Point Pelee is this amazing peninsula that juts out into Lake Erie. It is a major migratory corridor for birds — three hundred sixty species — and butterflies, on the southernmost point of mainland Canada. It's a biologist's dream, and getting to traipse around recording Indigo Buntings ranked right up there with chocolate ice cream and key lime pie for me.

"Dear girl, you're getting into the habit of losing important pieces of your research."

When I first met Duncan I had spent considerable energy trying to get him to stop calling me "dear girl," but either his brain was irreversibly programmed or he chose to ignore me because I was the one who had had to give in.

"He's got a point," said Martha, corralling my brain back to the present for a split second.

I thought back to the first murder Duncan, Martha, and I had worked on together and the research disks that had been stolen from the lab. This was different though. It had been my fault this time. I'd lost my keys somewhere not long before the car was stolen but hadn't panicked because I had a spare set hidden on the outside of the car. The thief could have discovered either set.

I sighed. "Well, I'll need to replace the lost recordings of the ten birds I taped at Point Pelee. I guess there is nothing for it. I'll just have to go back this week, if I can somehow reschedule all my other commitments." I really didn't want to go back and redo what I had done, but there seemed to be no other choice.

I left them talking on the porch and went and looked in the fridge. Cheese. A leftover loaf of bread. That was it. But I had an idea. I ducked out the back door and walked down the lane to the barn. I could hear Duncan and Martha talking on the porch and felt warm and safe as the sun made its way toward the horizon, pulling the night behind it. The escarpment at the back of my property was already in shadow as I pulled open the barn door. The cows rustled in their stalls and I knew my brother, Ryan, was somewhere in the barn milking cows. As kids we had sometimes competed against each other to see who could milk the most cows. Ryan usually won, but I secretly believed that he never emptied his cows' udders. Those were the days before the newfangled vacuum-extraction method of milking. I made my way down the length of the stalls, each one full of a thousand pounds of cow, to the far corner of the barn where we had a small henhouse. I opened the door and was hit by the stench that chickens just seem to make no matter how clean the coop. I collected a dozen eggs, still warm, and headed to the back of my house where I picked a selection of lettuce, peppers, onions, and carrots. Eating off the land. It felt good, and the salad and omelette that we ate on the porch tasted like the summer sun — light and hot.

We were all watching the bobolinks in the field when Duncan cleared his throat.

"What IS your research with the bird song, and why are your lost recordings so important?" he said.

I wiped my mouth with my napkin. "I needed them as baseline data for song dialects for my new experiments that will also deal with the anatomy of singing."

"Dialects?" asked Duncan.

"Yeah. Some birds sing in dialects. An Indigo Bunting in Kingston will sing a different version of the song than one in western Ontario."

"Like English and cockney English?"

"Exactly. The young birds hear the male singing and pattern their song after him. His song will vary from the birds some distance away and dialects form. I've already got songs from eastern Ontario. Point Pelee was the other location. I'm going to compare the differences and catalogue the notes and then move on to the anatomy."

"And how the devil do you do that — the identifying the bird by ear part?" asked Duncan. "You must have one hell of a good ear."

Martha sniggered and I said, "Well, actually, I'm pretty close to being tone deaf."

"Then my question stands."

"It's pretty simple. I suss them out by sight if I can, and go on a wing and a prayer if I can't. Then I just record the bird's song and convert it electronically into a sonogram, which is essentially the musical score of the bird's song."

"Like sheet music?" asked Duncan.

"Like sheet music but prettier to look at. You get blips and blobs and short fat notes and small, skinny ones and intricate lacework. Not all the same round dots that our music has. It's actually pretty cool. The chickadee, for instance, says chick-a-dee-dee-dee, which sounds simple but its sonogram is surprisingly complex."

"So why can't you choose an entirely different location for your second population of birds? It doesn't have to be Point Pelee does it?" said Duncan.

I cocked my head and looked at him. "What do you mean?"

"Exactly what I said. Another location where buntings are present."

"Did you have something in mind?"

"Spaniel Island."

"Which is where?"

"It's a small barrier island off the coast of South Carolina. There's a biology research station there," Duncan said as he mopped up the rest of his salad dressing with the bread.

"What's a barrier island?" Martha asked.

"It acts as a barrier between the sea and the mainland, catching the brunt of the wind and the waves."

"How do you know about this place?" I asked.

"I have a cottage on the island. I just came back from there a couple of weeks ago. I'm sure I could get you accommodation at the research station. Failing that, there is room in my cottage for you, but it would be more interesting at the research station. I know they have a vacant cabin because a researcher had to back out just this week. Shall I call them?"

Duncan was full of surprises. A cottage? On a barrier island? I looked at Martha, who shrugged and said, "Sounds like a good idea. It's a new location. You won't get frustrated over having to do it all again in the same place."

"But I don't have any equipment. It was all in the car. The tape recorder, the parabola, everything." *Besides*, I thought, *why would I want to go to a barrier island in the heat of summer, even if buntings were there?*

"I can check and see if the research station has any of that equipment. I know they have quite a bit of stuff." Duncan grabbed the bridge of his nose between his thumb and forefinger and pinched it. He was actually a good-looking older guy, if you could ignore his nose, which I couldn't, although his fine head of silver-grey hair and grey-blue eyes, which constantly smiled, almost competed.

"It won't cost you much either, Cordi. The station is subsidized," he said.

Looking back, all I know for sure is that I'm glad I didn't know the real price I would have to pay, or I never would have gone.

chapter two

Fortunately it was summer. Classes were out and I had some open time to redo my experiments, once I'd rescheduled some meetings. I rationalized that I would have had to take the time to go back to Pelee if Duncan hadn't come through with Spaniel Island, so it wasn't as if I was taking a vacation. It would be legitimate research. And Duncan, miraculously, had secured the recording equipment I would need to tape my birds. I wasn't even going to have to lug it with me. It was already down there. It would be fun to be at a research station again. There's something invigorating about the high-intensity atmosphere of such a place, where research is paramount and everyone is tied together to one common goal — to find answers to their questions. The questions, of course, are all different but the route to the answer lies in the heart and in the drive to do it, and researchers the world over have that in spades. If they don't they won't last.

The flight to Savannah was uneventful, although I was a little surprised when Martha showed up at the airport with a bag almost as big as she was and announced herself by calling out across fifty yards of airport that she was here and had managed to get a seat beside me. Don't get me wrong. Martha and I are good friends. It's just that I hadn't known that she was coming with me. She had neglected to mention that when she booked the tickets.

"Duncan invited me down. Although I told him I wanted to stay at the research station with you, rather than with him. Hard decision, but you're going to need me as a research assistant to help with all those little buntings," she said, daring me to contradict her.

The fact that I hadn't needed her at Point Pelee didn't seem to have crossed her mind. She told me once that she hated the wilderness and this island was going to be pretty wild, if I knew Duncan. *What people do for their lovers*, I thought and then winced. My erstwhile lover, Patrick, had flown across the pond to take a job in London, England. I hadn't been willing to give up my career to follow him and he hadn't been willing to give up his. We had seen each other just once in the last eight months. I had new respect for Martha, to overcome her dislike of the wilderness because she loved Duncan that much.

We had to change planes in Atlanta. Our connecting plane was a tiny twenty-seat affair, and as it sat on the tarmac I looked out the window and watched a couple of men manhandle Martha's suitcase into the hold. We were only in the air for forty minutes and landed at a tiny airport on the coast. From there we had to take a taxi, which proved problematic as we tried to stuff Martha's suitcase in the trunk. In the end it had to go in the backseat. The taxi driver talked nonstop all the way to the wharf, where a boat was waiting to take us to the island. The wharf had seen better days and parts of it were plastered with seagull poop. The birds themselves had taken up perches on the tops of masts and bridges, watching guard over their domain, ever ready should a child drop a French fry or a fisherman unload some fish guts overboard. The marina was located up a tidal creek from the sea, so there were no breathtaking vistas or pounding waves, only a mediocre working marina catering to the sailors and captains of smaller vessels. It was actually anticlimactic.

We made our way down the dock to our boat — a large open wooden vessel with an enclosed front half that looked sturdy enough to easily manage rough seas. A black-haired, bearded middle-aged man had the hatch to the engine open amidships and was fiddling with something inside, a look of concentration on his face. When we hove in view the look turned to impending impatience. When I said, "Hello. Is this the boat to Spaniel Island?" he just grunted and went on with his repair work with a desultory wave of the hand, which I took to mean "Yes." I must say it didn't instill a great deal of confidence seeing all those tools laid out on the deck and the sweat on his brow. But it all washed over Martha, who started up a one-sided conversation with the man. While she was talking at him a very tall, very thin man wearing a forest green hoodie that half covered his face arrived and eyeballed the tools, and Martha and the captain.

"Looks like you need a hand, Trevor," he said.

"In more ways than one," growled Trevor. "Welcome back, David," he added, but with gritted teeth.

"Still haven't come around yet, huh?" asked David. When Trevor didn't respond he said, "And here I thought you'd actually taken a liking to sea turtles." And he laughed, but without any humour.

Trevor didn't answer this cryptic comment but instead scowled, got up, returned his tools to a toolbox, and went up to the bow of the boat. Seconds later the engine coughed to life and Trevor released his lines and we were off. While the marina had been nothing to write home about, where we were going was quite another story. We motored into the inland waterway separating the mainland from the barrier islands and the Atlantic Ocean. There was a swell as we rounded a headland into the open ocean between two barrier islands and I felt my stomach begin to lurch. I had visions of myself aboard the *Susanna Moodie*, the ship that had taken me to the Arctic the previous summer and had left murder and mayhem in its wake, along with nauseatingly horrible seasickness. I tried to calm down by reminding myself that it was only a half-hour trip, or so Duncan had said. We were headed toward a long narrow island that danced in the distance, its white-sand beaches taking up the sun and flinging it back in a brilliance of dazzling light. I concentrated on that and the queasiness subsided. As we drew closer the island came into focus, the dark green of the live oaks in sharp contrast to the white of the beaches.

"I wonder why they call it Spaniel Island?" asked Martha. It was a rhetorical question that to our surprise actually garnered an answer. David had materialized at our sides and was gazing at the island with what looked like relish, his green hoodie now thrown back to reveal a circle of bright white hair outlining the bald spot on the top of his head. When he saw us looking at him he rearranged his long thin face and aquiline nose to look more or less neutral. I wondered why he had bothered.

"It's the quintessential story of a dog and a boy," he said. "Originally the island was called Little Island, rather unimaginative, if not descriptive. It is actually only ten kilometers long and maybe a kilometer wide, off its diet."

He leaned against the railing of the boat and continued. "It was 1949. A mother and father and their three young children and the family Springer Spaniel were on the beach." He pointed to the island. "See? The south end on the sea side. They had found a nice place on the white sands, very close to where a tidal creek penetrated into the island. It's actually still there today. When the tide is going out these creeks become fast moving rivers. The little boy, the youngest, crawled over to the creek and the sandy embankment gave way and he fell in."

Martha's face was illustrating every detail of the story and I almost laughed, but it wasn't exactly the right moment to do that.

"The tide was going out, and the little boy was being carried out to sea and was going under. The parents couldn't swim. That's when the spaniel catapulted himself into the creek and swam to the child, grabbing it by the back of his T-shirt and swimming with the current until it was weak enough to let the dog and the boy cross over to some islands of sand that had been exposed by the tides. It was a little miracle and the powers that be renamed the island in honour of the spaniel."

"Why didn't they name it after the animal's actual name?" said Martha, her face a mixture of worry, indignation, and joy.

"Because the animal was named Bunchkins," said David as he reached back and pulled the hoodie up over his head. The wind had sprung up and I wished I had a hoodie too.

We stood in companionable silence for a while, and then I said, "What brings you to Spaniel Island?"

He looked at me, his eyebrows almost meeting as they rose in a quizzical salute, as if he was trying to size me up. "I'd like to say that I come here quite often to rejuvenate, which is true, but this time I am here on some unpleasant business. In such a place of beauty it seems a shame that the banalities of life should intrude."

I couldn't think of anything to say to that little bomb and, in fact, he didn't let me. He wanted to know why we were here. After I told him he chuckled. "I hope you don't think it will be a vacation rooming in with that lot."

Hearing him call my research a vacation grated on me, but I let it go. Instead I said, "You know them?"

He chuckled again and the smile on his face was not soft and warming — it was jeering and predatory and it made me very uncomfortable. "All a bunch of prima donnas," he said and glanced at me again as if to say "Are you one too?"

I tried to imagine a research station full of prima donnas and couldn't. Biologists may be eccentric, even opinionated, but most of them would not be classified as prima donnas. Although, maybe not. He seemed to be reading my mind.

"All right. Not ALL prima donnas. But they are a strong bunch of individuals and they make me uncomfortable always talking about their research as if it was the only thing on earth." Did I detect a hint of anger in his voice?

"They're just a harmless and dedicated bunch of biologists," Martha said helpfully. I glowered at her. She had just pigeonholed my life in one lighthearted sentence.

"Dedicated? Yes," he said and turned to stare at us. "But harmless? No."

chapter three

We came into the interior of the island through a tidal creek that meandered and wound its way through the glistening of exposed mud banks — the tide was falling and the tall, thick reeds that lined the banks as far as the eye could see were giving up the secret places where little crabs and other crustaceans took refuge. The creek was narrow and the current was fast and it took some skill to drive the boat without bashing into a mud bank. The reeds encompassed us so that we could no longer see the island. We were essentially in a wandering maze, only the cobalt blue sky to show us there was another world outside the reeds. And then we broke out of the reeds to the higher ground of the island proper and the end of the tidal creek. After we landed at a rickety wooden dock, built on stilts to allow for the tides, we found ourselves in a relatively treeless area, on bare, compact sand with numerous buildings spread about — mostly sheds and garages — and lots of ATVs. It was really quite ugly and I wondered what I had got myself into. Trevor had scooted off the boat with lightning speed, after a lightning fast "Welcome to the Compound" speech, and disappeared into one of the outbuildings. But David stood nearby, presumably waiting for a ride, just as we were.

Even at 6:00 at night it was blisteringly hot. The tangy smell of the salt mixed with the pungent decaying smell of the mud and the ugliness of the landing area made it difficult to believe that this was, in fact, a beautiful island, or so Duncan had said. Martha and I found a tiny scrap of shade to hide in and waited. We heard them before we saw them — the unmistakable roar of engines with mufflers no longer used to heavy labour. It wasn't long before two ATVs came barrelling around one of the sheds and stopped in front of David, who was lounging against a picnic table incongruously placed so it had a view of one of the sheds. David slowly rose to his feet as a woman with gossamer blonde hair and a scary pale face extricated her considerable girth from one of the ATVs and glanced over at David before taking in Martha and me and our luggage. "Good thing we brought the trailer," she said.

I glanced at the ATVs. One of them was pulling a rusty, dilapidated, old wooden trailer. It didn't take a calculator to see that two large women, me, David, our luggage, and the other driver were going to tax the taxi service. And I knew what that meant. Being the smallest, I'd get the trailer. The other driver waved at us as he got off the ATV and walked out of sight behind one of the sheds. I watched in curiosity as the woman more or less ignored us and limped over to welcome David, cane in hand but not being used. She stood square in front of him for a long time, seemingly searching his face for something, before abruptly reaching out and giving him a hug. David stiffened at first and then melted into the hug as if they had been doing this dance all their lives. I wondered how they knew each other, this tall thin man and this tall fat woman.

Before I could muse on this question any longer David called over to us. "Meet Stacey. The best damned researcher this side of the picnic table." We stared at him and he laughed. Stacey was frowning but then finally found her manners and we all shook hands.

"You're the Indigo Bunting lady, right?" Her voice was soft and high, like a flute on the wind. It seemed at odds with her large size.

I nodded.

"Been here before?" She was holding her cane in her right hand, as if she was about to stab someone with it. It was an odd way to hold a cane.

"No."

"Only two real rules. One: make sure you know the location of everyone's study site. We don't want you barging in where you aren't wanted." Which sounded as though it was everywhere by the tone of her voice. "And two: never ever break the first rule." For some reason she made me feel as though I was back in kindergarten and getting my knuckles rapped — metaphorically speaking of course — by the time I arrived in kindergarten they had long since stopped rapping little knuckles. I wondered what her research project was. You can tell a lot about a scientist by what they are studying. I realized in hindsight that it would have been a good idea to get a list of all the people and their research projects. I'd have to search them on the Internet. I had been told there was Internet on the island. I just hoped it was high speed. Stacey motioned for us to load our luggage and, as Martha and I struggled with Martha's suitcase, she and David stood huddled together.

It seems we were waiting for the second driver.

"Shit's going to hit the fan now he's here." He'd sneaked up on us and I jumped a mile. I looked at the driver, whose flamboyant hat was hard on the eyes — crimson and royal blue with a lime green logo of a pelican in flight. I thought at first he was about fifteen, but his close-cropped brown hair was beginning to thin so I had to revise my estimate upward to maybe twenty-five.

"What shit?" I asked, knowing he was counting on me to ask. I mean, it was like a red flag waving at a bull. It would have been hard not to.

"Always hits the fan when those two are together. They love to hate each other." I glanced over at Stacey and David. He was handing her a yellow envelope. She was gripping his shoulder and what little blood had been in her face to begin with had drained away. She dropped her hand and leaned over the picnic table as if she was catching her breath.

"Darcy," said the man beside me, as if he was talking about buying a head of lettuce. I looked down at him; he was a good four inches shorter than I was.

"Pardon?"

"The name's Darcy. Who might you be?"

I introduced Martha and myself.

"Right. The Bunting Lady. Well. Welcome. As you can see, Stacey isn't much of a social coordinator. That's why I came along."

I bit my tongue and did not point out to him that he had skedaddled as soon as he arrived and that Stacey had at least stayed put.

He laughed. "Had to pee."

I looked at him in astonishment.

"What else could you have been thinking?" He laughed again. "Aren't you going to ask me what I do?"

"What do you do?"

"I'm Stacey's assistant."

"And what do you assist her with?"

"Flowers, plants, grasses, admin stuff ..."

So she's a botanist, I thought. Methodical, detailed. And probably not a risk-taker, at least not in the field.

I was about to ask what she was working on, but he broke in. "Better get those two back to the research station before they either kill each other with affection or with venom." David and Stacey were hugging again. He winked at me and called over to Stacey to get a leg on, which seemed a little cruel given the state of one of her legs.

As I had expected, I got the trailer. I arranged myself well away from Martha's killer luggage. One wild ride around a corner and it was likely to pinion me. We were barely out of the compound when the island showed its other face, the one you want to look at and live with forever.

It was a riotous mass of towering live oaks and hip-high palmetto, where the roads were mere trails, packed sand carpeted with live oak leaves. You could almost see the breadcrumbs if you tried hard enough. It was easy to imagine that nothing had changed on this island since the days of Columbus. No signs of civilization except for the trails. Not even electrical or telephone wires marred the view. I lay back against the head of the trailer and looked up at the magnificent oaks, leaves carving a lacey pattern in the sky. As we drove down the trails the only thing out of place with this timeless, ageless island were the ATVs.

My reverie was broken by Martha, who was yelling at me. "Darcy says the island residents formed a co-operative and designed the development to have a tiny environmental footprint. No paved roads, underground hydro wires, and none of the cottages are allowed to be seen from the beach."

It took her multiple tries to get this across to me above the roar of the ATVs, which were certainly not environmentally friendly. But the underground wires were good, and the prohibition on building anything with a sea view was pretty impressive. I wondered how many of the co-operative had railed against that. I was lost in thinking about myself walking down this trail at the dawn of time, when the ATV screeched to a halt and Darcy pointed at something ahead of us. I had to squint because it was pretty small, whatever it was, but as the vehicles inched closer I saw it was an armadillo, that very prehistoric looking creature with the funny back. It meandered across the road, looking lost and vaguely like Piglet with a set of armor. It scurried into the palmetto and was lost to sight. But we could still hear it rustling, the same way its ancestors had done for countless generations. What is it that makes the passing of time, huge amounts of it, seem so sad and melancholy? Is it that such vast amounts of time are something we can never know and bridging the gulf between our own small lives and eternity is impossible? We can only imagine. *Wow*,

I thought. *This island is pretty powerful.* Not that my musings really hold much water. It's a barrier island after all, and barrier islands come and go, shaped by the wind and the ocean's currents. Regardless, this island had been around longer than I had, and the armadillo's ancestors were older than mine.

I spent the rest of the trip watching the live oaks recede down the trail and was somehow disappointed when we reached our destination. I shouldn't have been though. It was pretty impressive and not what I had imagined at all. In my head I had seen the station overlooking the sea, but since this wasn't allowed I had altered my vision to match the ugly one we had seen at the compound. The research station was a series of tasteful wooden buildings built seemingly at random among the live oaks that soared overhead. But the centre of attention was a large wooden staircase that snaked its way up the face of a dune to a handsome log building that poked its roof out through the canopy. I had read up a bit on barrier islands and this one was essentially long and narrow. Behind the beach, which we hadn't seen yet, were a series of dunes that marched inland. The further inland they were the more clothed in vegetation they became. It was this vanguard of dunes that the large building was perched on, its underbelly exposed to anyone looking up at it. Apparently the island residents had been loath to cut down any trees, because everything seemed positioned so as to avoid any of the trees. Or so I surmised.

There was a whole bevy of ATVs at the bottom of the main staircase, like a miniature army taking a break in operations. It was dinnertime. We could hear voices wafting on the breeze — the windows were all open. I was hot and sticky and cranky and feeling decidedly unenvironmental, and open windows meant no air conditioning. Stacey made way for Darcy and the trailer, with me still in it, and he pulled up in front of the stairs to the dining room. As soon as he stopped, in the still evening air a horde of no-see-ums descended on us and my skin began to itch all over. No-see-ums, punkies, sand flies — those irascible insects, with their gigantic jaws, that are no bigger than a grain of salt — the entire insect, not the jaws. If you've never met a punkie you would swear you had some awful itching rash or worse, because they are really hard to see. In fact there's a story about two medical students on a wilderness trip in Newfoundland who actually thought they had come down with some exotic and nasty disease after being bitten by no-see-ums. They cut short their trip and made a beeline for the nearest emergency room where they were laughed all the way out of the waiting room.

We went up those stairs faster than they deserved — as I sprinted by I could tell they were beautifully made out of two-inch cedar — just to get out of the clutches of those swarming no-see-ums. Ah, the wilderness, blessed with beauty and cursed with biting insects. I shivered and raced into the dining room ahead of everyone. Unfortunately for me my entrance coincided with the moment when everyone was taking a break from talking, and they all stared at me as if I was an apparition. The ten seconds it took for Darcy to land at my side was an eternity, both to me and to them. Their curiosity was palpable.

But most of them lost interest and turned back to their meal when I didn't do a pirouette while standing on my hands. At least, that is, until Martha catapulted into the room, frantically waving her arms around and jerking her body about as if she was convulsing. She gave me a venomous look as if I had been the one to force her to come down here in the first place. Once again everyone was looking at us and I felt an overwhelming urge to stand on one of the tables and announce who Martha and I were. So I did. Not stand on the table, but I just bellowed out the news that I was a zoologist studying buntings and I looked forward to meeting everybody while I was here. I mean, no one else was introducing us. I had to break the ice somehow. I felt Martha clutching at my arm.

"Jesus, Cordi. What was that all about?"

"Just trying to be friendly."

"You never do that. Ever."

The building we stood in was a wooden panabode and it was dark, even though the sun was still high in the sky. The windows were small and there weren't many of them, and it was hot as hell in there. I could see sweat glistening on just about all the diners as the stark electric lights strung from the ceiling made a stab at turning the darkness into light. Six wooden picnic tables filled up most of the space but only two were full — the two farthest away from the hot kitchen. What with the cramped space I shuddered to think what it would be like when every seat was taken. The pungent smell of sweat was covering the smell of the food, but by the looks of it, it was some kind of fish. Actually, it didn't look half bad and I kind of wished I could smell it.

Darcy motioned us over to one of the tables. "This is the mess," he said. I surveyed the tables quickly. Two people deep in conversation occupied the one closest to me and I felt reluctant to interrupt, so I chose the other table. It was occupied by a diminutive redhead sporting a shiner that clashed with her hair. She seemed distracted, or maybe depressed. Whatever it was had made her face look sour and pinched. I wondered what could have happened to her. She was so young. Maybe twenty-three. Too young to be embittered, surely? She was sitting alone at our end of the table, as if by choice, and at the far end was a man who was engrossed in a magazine with the headline: "Sex and Lies." Stocky, plain looking with unkempt, long, straggly black hair and a heavy beard shadow, he didn't seem the type to be reading a gossip rag.

My thoughts were interrupted by Darcy, who plunked two laden dishes down on the table in front of us, right next to the woman, and went back to get something for himself.

I glanced at the woman sitting right beside me, and said, "Mind if we join you?"

She glanced up and gave me a fleeting smile, and I could see that the shiner was accompanied by some big-time swelling.

"Looks painful," I said, shamelessly fishing for information.

"I banged into my cabin door," she said, staring at me, seemingly daring me to contradict her. I wouldn't have even thought to contradict her except for the pleading look in her eyes that was there only for an instant and then it was gone. So fast I couldn't really be sure it had been there at all, so I ignored it.

"I'm Cordi. And this is Martha."

"Yeah, I know," she said.

Right, I'd already forgotten my earlier *episode*. I held out my hand.

"Rosemary Nesbitt." She gripped my hand without much interest. She was obviously somewhere far away and Martha and I had interrupted her.

"So I see you have met Rosemary!" Darcy placed his tray across from us and sat down.

"She's our resident vet-in-training. Singlehandedly nursed a baby armadillo back to health." Darcy's smile was big and broad, but oddly disconcerting. I looked at Rosemary. She was staring at him, the way one stares at something of little interest, but he ignored her and said, "Rosemary is in her third year of vet school and ..."

"Fourth and last year," interrupted Rosemary. She turned and looked at me then. "I'm here helping to vaccinate the female wild horses so they can't get pregnant."

I hadn't heard of such a thing and I said so.

"It's a small island and the horses can do tremendous damage, grazing the dunes. The herd here is already too big, but no one wants to cull them. This seemed like a good compromise. Give them PZP."

"PZP?" I asked.

"Porcine zona pellucida. It's an immunocontraceptive vaccine." Rosemary sighed. "Anyway, there are a number of island residents who are vehemently opposed to this vaccination. They feel we should be leaving things to nature."

"Only nature never envisioned horses on this island," said Darcy. "The Spanish released some horses in the 1500s on the much bigger island to the north of us and now the herd there numbers about two hundred or so. Right, Rosemary?"

It was interesting seeing Darcy's technique to draw Rosemary into the conversation, but it seemed to work. Her eyes had come afire and she was tracing her hands through the air to punctuate what she was saying. "That island is big enough to accommodate the horses. But this island is too small. They figure the horses got here in the first place by swimming across the channel. No other way they could have come. So now it is crucial to preserve island habitat. The horses are considered exotic or weed species that are not endemic to the area. But that doesn't seem to matter to some of the islanders."

"Is that where you got your black eye?" It just came out of my mouth without warning.

She swivelled to look at me and said in a clipped tongue, "I thought I told you it was my cabin door." End of conversation.

chapter four

Rosemary ate in silence, and when she was finished she got up without a word, nodded her head at me, and went to join the man reading the gossip rag. Darcy and Martha were deep in conversation about something, so I finished my meal and thought about getting up for some more. At that moment the screen door of the mess room squeaked open and Stacey walked in, or rather staggered. She was sweating copiously and her face was an unhealthy pasty grey. I wondered how she had managed the stairs with her gimpy leg and her excess pounds. She looked like a heart attack waiting to happen. She surveyed the room in what I can only describe as controlled panic. Hiding something, but not very successfully. She remained standing at the door and said, "May I have your attention, please?" The buzz of conversation slowly petered out, as she accepted a glass of water from Darcy, who had darted out of his seat to help her.

"As you all know, we enjoy the use of these research facilities because of the islanders. As director of this research facility, I must remind you that if we lose their trust we lose this station. The islanders voted for the vaccination of the horses, and for this reason we must support that decision and help Wyatt and Rosemary do their job."

Who was Wyatt? I wondered.

Stacey continued. "It has come to my attention that someone among you has tried to sabotage the vaccine."

The room had gone quiet, the way a room can when those in it have all been accused of a crime. *What a time to be visiting the island*, I thought.

"Can you tell us the details?" asked David.

Stacey looked around and sighed. "Apparently, some of the vaccine has gone missing. Is a Dr. Wyatt Sinclair here?" I followed her gaze around the room. A man sitting at the far back gestured with his hand. He was, for lack of a better word, an impressive looking man, with a head of wildly thick white hair that cascaded over half of his very expansive forehead and accented the startling blue of his eyes. He exuded a self-confidence that was apparent even before he spoke. He rose to his feet, laughed a hollow laugh, and said, "Will the perpetrator please stand up now so that we can get on with our job?"

No one stood up. "Worth a try," he said, but the way he had said it left no doubt that he wanted his vaccine back. "Seriously, someone had the gall to let themselves into my cabin yesterday and steal a bottle of vaccine that was on my desk. This is totally unacceptable, and I need it back." He scanned the room, his face unreadable, and then suddenly he smiled, a charming cat-in-the-cream sort of smile, at Stacey, who had a queer look on her face, as if she was going to be sick.

"Why are you singling us out for sabotage? I mean, there are islanders who don't want this to happen." The deep, guttural voice came from the dark-haired man sitting beside Rosemary.

Wyatt bowed to Stacey. Stacey hesitated, her face quickly suffused with blood and her eyes clouded. The confusion on her face was intriguing.

"I am aware of that, Sam," she finally said in a quiet voice. "But the easiest route is usually the correct route, and all of us here in this room would have an easier time sabotaging the vaccine than any islander."

The buzz of conversation that followed this comment was cut short by Stacey, who said in a tight, pained voice that matched her face, "You know who you are, and when you are caught we will prosecute to the fullest extent of the law." As she hurriedly turned toward the kitchen her face seemed to collapse in on itself as if the weight of the world was just too much. She seemed so alone and vulnerable. I wondered if she counted any of the people present as her friend. She seemed like she could use one.

Darcy interrupted my thoughts to say that he and Martha would be back in a minute; he had to show her something before showing us to our cabin. It never ceased to amaze me at how fast Martha could make friends, and have them eating out of her hands. But I'd had about enough excitement for one day and they were gone longer than I wanted. Finally, Darcy led Martha and me back into the no-see-ums, down the stairs, and then over to a little cabin tucked in between two honking big live oaks. Martha was lugging her huge suitcase behind her and was breathing heavily by the time we got to the cabin. It was even tinier than it looked. There was just enough room for two beds and a night table, one chest of drawers, a desk, and a chair. No washroom. As if reading my mind, Darcy, who was standing in the doorway, said, "They skimped on the bathrooms. The woman's is one over from the mess stairs." He laughed. "Just don't get the trots."

Martha rolled her eyes as Darcy pushed past us, plunked himself down on one of the beds, and bounced up and down. "At least the mattresses in this cabin are okay." Which gave me visions of lumpy pretzel mattresses that sagged and smelled in some of the other cabins. I wondered who got those.

"So what's all this about the vaccine being stolen?" I asked.

"Tempest in a teapot. Wyatt probably just misplaced it. Or maybe he didn't bring as much as he thought he had. It'll quiet down. It always does."

He got up from the bed and I wondered why he seemed so sure — or was he? He actually seemed a bit too glib. And what was this *always does* all about?

"Is Wyatt a regular?" I asked.

Darcy laughed. "No, he's here on a working vacation. He's a first timer angling to be a last timer, judging by his attitude. He's not a researcher and he likes to make that pretty clear. He's a prickly guy, always complaining about something. And he and Jayne are always goading each other."

"Who's Jayne?" I asked.

"She's our turtle lady. Does research on sea turtles. She used to be the director until she retired and Stacey took over. Everybody said it was because Jayne burned out. Too bad really — at least for Jayne. I think she genuinely liked being director."

"And Stacey doesn't?"

He cocked his head at me and smiled. "Did I say that?"

When I didn't say anything he got up off the bed and said, "Breakfast is at 7:30. Don't be late or you won't get anything." And with that he was gone.

It didn't take long for me to unpack. I sat on my bed and watched Martha trying to stuff all her clothes into two of the four drawers. I finally took pity on her and gave her one of mine. However, the suitcase and the remainder of her clothes we had to leave between the two beds because there was nowhere else to put them.

"What did you think of Darcy?" I asked innocently.

"Salesman par excellence," said Martha and laughed.

"Yeah, that's what I thought. The guy everyone loves because he makes you feel good. So what is he doing as an assistant to a botanist, of all things?"

"He's young. Couldn't be more than twenty-five. Maybe he's just trying out his wings. After all, if he can ingratiate himself with this ragtag bunch of people he'd make a hell of an event planner," said Martha.

"Or maybe there's more to it than that."

"Oh, Cordi, there you go, glass half empty. How can you read anything negative in Darcy? And why ever would you want to? He's a gem."

I stared at Martha, realizing that she had a point. Except that ever since I had stepped on this island I had felt like I was in a glass house. One move and it would all shatter around me in so many lethal shards. I shivered. It was a weird sensation and I didn't like it one bit.

"Good lord, Cordi. How can you be cold in weather like this?" She slung an unfamiliar camera over her shoulder and headed for the door, followed by my raised eyebrow. "Darcy lent me a night-vision camera. I have to check it out." It didn't seem to matter to her that it wasn't dark outside yet.

I lay in bed for a long time, listening to the sounds of the woods and the chirruping of frogs, until I finally fell asleep to the wind whispering through the trees.

I was jerked awake by the sound of firecrackers going off. After I picked myself up from where I had plastered myself to the ground, I traced the unearthly racket back to Martha, who was snoring shotguns on every breath in. Too bad she couldn't be as quiet sleeping as she obviously was coming home from her photography junket. The one other time I'd spent the night with Martha I hadn't remembered that she snored. *Must be a new thing*, I thought.

After that I didn't sleep much, and by the time I'd watched my clock tick through from 3:00 to 5:00 I'd had enough. The darkness had given way to dawn and I could just make out the trunk of the oak outside my window. I took my time getting dressed and then fished out my flashlight and tiptoed out the door, though why I bothered to be quiet I don't know. Martha was making more noise than I ever could.

Because my cabin, along with all the others, had been built at the base of a dune line it felt as though I was in a valley as I walked outside, a valley with hills covered in palmetto — a miniature palm tree, three or four feet high, with fingered fronds just like the bigger palms, hence palmetto or "little palm." As I stood there, looking up the side of the enormous dune upon which the main building stood, I saw the pale grey of early morning topping the rise, peeking out between the latticework of the oak branches. Everywhere I looked were live oaks, wispy pale green strands of hanging moss clinging to their branches like hair.

"You're up early."

I spun around at the sound of the voice, my heart racing. In the dim light he was hard to make out. His jet-black hair was tied back now and he was dressed as if for a fall day, with a long-sleeved black shirt buttoned right to the neck, like a nerd. And like a nerd his trouser legs were tucked into his socks. As he came closer I caught the distinct smell of perfume. I thought I must be mistaken, but when he stopped in front of me all I could smell was the scent of a woman's cologne. I don't like to think I'm prejudiced but I almost took one step back because it was so unexpected.

"My name's Sam," he said and held out his hand. It was gnarled and calloused, a working man's hand. Definitely not the hand of a man who wears women's perfume.

I gripped it and said, "Cordi."

I could see now that he had a mist net slung over his shoulder and he was carrying a yellow toolbox with the black silhouette of a bat stamped on its top. Not a bird man then.

"Bats?" I asked.

He smiled. "You got it. I'm studying the parasites of the big brown bat."

I wondered what it said about the man that he had chosen a nocturnal mammal to study. When everyone else was asleep he would be awake and vice versa. A man who either did not need the company of other people or a man living his life as an outcast, but not by choice. Of course, there was a third possibility that Martha would definitely point out to me had she been there: a man simply doing research on an animal he found irresistible.

"Do you mist net them at their roost?" I asked as I eyeballed the net over his shoulder. Mist nets are gossamer-thin nets used to capture birds, and in this case bats, so that they can be tagged and their behaviour studied.

He shifted the mist net on his shoulder. "The area around the roost is the easiest place to capture them as they leave to go hunting for the night, or come back in the morning, but there's a danger of catching too many. I'll show you if you want? It's not far from here."

His vehicle was a modified golf cart with a two-person front seat, and I settled in beside him as the engine coughed to life. I imagined many hearts in the various cabins jumping to attention at the sound of that motor and hoped that none of them were weak. We drove out of what Darcy had called the clearing — the more-or-less empty area that surrounded the research station on three sides — and down the leaf-lined, sandy road through a tunnel of trees. It was still dark here, but when I looked up the sky was turning blue.

The road wound its way through the forest, the wheels leaving no marks on the compacted sand. Sam pulled into a dent in the forest and got out of the cart. I followed and he led me along a sandy path, palmetto encroaching on all sides and overhead the ubiquitous oaks. And then we broke out into the open.

"Beach is just over that dune line," he said. But I wasn't looking at that. I was looking at the burnt-out wreck of an abandoned building, its skeleton and intact roof still reaching for the sky as sand from a naked sand dune spilled down into its foundation like the sand from an hourglass finally set free.

"We've missed them. They've already come home."

I looked at the building and wondered who had once made their home here, besides the bats. There was a sign hanging by one black chain at the front door that said HUNTER'S and I could almost imagine the laughter and the fun they had once had here.

"C'mon — we might just catch the sunrise." Sam was striding past the building and into the valley between two dunes. I had to run to keep up. And then there it was.

We topped a dune and the beach stretched in both directions, vast and mysterious, primeval, white, and empty of human life. And into the midst of this incredible beauty the sun had risen just above the ocean's horizon, red and distinct as if someone had cut a hole in the sky to let it shine through. But it wasn't shining yet. It was still blood red and flat, and you could look at it without hurting your eyes. It all seemed out of time. This is what it could have been like millions of years ago, when some other creature stood here and looked at the sun.

We didn't say anything. We just stared at the red ball as it turned into an orange orb of flame, at the blue of the sea and the jagged crests of the waves, at the shifting sands and the pelicans flying low to the water. Surely such moments as these are what we live for, what keeps us going until the next one? You share something like that with a stranger and they are strangers no longer.

In silence we walked down to the water's edge, the white sand now stained dark by the sea — the tide was going out. I turned and looked back at where we had come from but there was no sign of Hunter's, just the dazzling white of the dunes marching inward to be clothed by trees. I looked all down the shoreline and there weren't any cottages to be seen from the beach. It felt as though we were the only two people on the entire island — in the entire world.

"Pretty amazing, isn't it?" said Sam. "It seems incredible that such an eclectic bunch of islanders could get together and agree on how to conserve this island so well."

"How does it work? Do they own the land?"

"The land was divided up into one hundred lots and each lot was sold to pay for the price of the island. They have a board of directors and a set of bylaws and each resident has one voting share. Everything is done democratically, so nobody can complain that something has been foisted on them. But it makes for some fireworks when there is disagreement."

"You mean like the horses?"

"Yeah. Some of the islanders feel that the horses are a natural part of the island and should be allowed to procreate. They feel strongly that this is the philosophy of the island — to let things take their course."

"But the horses are not endemic to the island?"

"No, but the islanders don't care. The horses got here through an act of God — a shipwreck — and therefore they are a natural part of the island. Or that is their philosophy."

"Is God a factor here?"

Sam laughed. "No more than anywhere else. I mean he always pops up, doesn't he? Even among a group of people trained in science."

His comment begged a question.

"Who?"

Sam laughed. "Well now, I don't like to gossip, but our esteemed director is a devout Catholic."

I wasn't sure how to answer that one and he continued, "Tricky situation for her. She believes in the conservation of the island but how does she square her Catholicism to birth control for horses? Or does her religion spread that far?"

"Fortunately for her," I said, "it's all moot."

"Why's that?" Sam looked puzzled.

"Well, she doesn't have a voting share, so there are no worries."

"Actually, you're wrong. She owns a cottage on the island. Bought it last year. So she is very much in the thick of things here."

"And which side has she weighed in on?"

Sam stared at me. "Dunno," he said gruffly, but I got the distinct impression he knew exactly what side she was on. He just wasn't going to tell me.

chapter five

———————————

Sam dropped me off at the stairs to the mess room and, in daylight, I climbed those countless steps in a twisty turny path to the top. It was pretty impressive now that the no-see-ums were gone and I could actually see. The main building, which housed the dining room, blended in like a Frank Lloyd Wright building and was bracketed by the branches of a dozen oak trees so that it looked like a treehouse of awesome proportions. I could see our cabin down in the large *U*-shaped clearing, or rather the pathway to it as the trees, with their cloaks of Spanish moss, hid the cabin from view. There were six or seven pathways into the bush, presumably leading to more cabins, and the clearing was partially filled with various vehicles. When I walked in the door of the dining room it took awhile to adjust to the light.

"Cordi!" shrieked someone from the gloaming. I squinted and saw Martha waving her hands up and down and pointing to the picnic table where she was sitting. I waved back and went and got myself some breakfast. It was a full logger's meal — bacon and eggs, hash browns, toast, pancakes, sausages. There was so much of it that I felt a little sick. I brought the plate over to Martha's table.

"Holy crap, Cordi. Where have you been? I wake up at 5:30 and you're not there!" She glared at me.

"Just out watching the sunrise with Sam," I said, and the woman across from me choked on her breakfast.

Martha glanced over. "Melanie, this is Cordi, my boss." Melanie was about nineteen years old, with a smooth, pale complexion and wild red and blue streaks in her blond hair. She was very thin, but the kind of thin that looked genetic rather than self-induced. Her cheeks were little hollows and her clothes hung loosely to her frame. I glanced at her breakfast plate. One apple and a glass of milk. *Could have been worse*, I thought.

Melanie was still trying to control her choking and flapped her hand around until she was able to say "Hi."

She was staring at me closely with a look of surprise on her face, making me feel most uncomfortable. "With Sam?" she asked, her voice croaking, but I couldn't tell whether it was from the choking or something else.

Oh, boy. Was I stepping on toes?

She recomposed herself and said, "He was supposed to meet me for breakfast, but I guess he forgot."

I looked at my watch; 7:35. He wasn't late by much if breakfast started at 7:30. As I started to sit down the squeak of the dining-room door alerted everyone and in walked Sam. Minus the shirt buttoned too high, and with his pant legs hanging over his boots, not tucked into them, he looked exceptionally masculine, his shirt opened to reveal a mass of curly black hair trying to escape. He nodded at us and went to get his breakfast. I looked at Melanie and she smiled back uncertainly.

"You're the birdsong lady," she said as Sam slipped in beside her and brushed her hand with his hand.

"That's right," I said. She flicked a strand of electric blue hair out of her eyes, as she moved her hand away from Sam's.

"What do you do?" I said.

"Snakes," she said. "Rattlesnakes." The way she said it reminded me of Bond, James Bond. But it also sounded like a taunt.

I took the bait. "How did someone like you come to pick rattlesnakes as a research topic?"

Her answer surprised me. "I was terrified of snakes. One of my questionable friends put a snake in my bed one night as a joke. Some joke. Have you any idea what it's like to be in bed and stretch out your feet, in that luxurious way you can only do in bed, and have this slithery creature dart over your feet?"

I was having a pretty good go at reenacting that scenario and gave an involuntary shudder. And I'm not even afraid of snakes.

"Exactly," she said. "So choosing to work with a venomous snake seemed like a good way to control my fear." I could think of other ways to do that — like avoiding them altogether.

"And did it work?"

"You can't spend hours milking a snake, looking at its fangs under a microscope, watching it eat, watching its habits, videotaping it, without developing respect for it and once you have respect the fear fades. Not completely

— these are venomous creatures — but it fades to a normal level. I mean, if you're not afraid of venomous snakes you'd better take out a life-insurance policy. As for non-venomous snakes — they're a breeze now."

She smiled at Sam, her face lighting up, but even as it did she clamped down and the smile altered, the warmth draining from it to be replaced by something unidentifiable. I followed her gaze and saw Stacey, food tray in hand, coming over to join us. She really was a big woman, not big boned, just plain and simple fat. In all my years as a zoologist I had never met a fat scientist. She still looked like hell, only worse. The only colour in her face was her tiny perfect lips. Several rolls of fat bracketed her chin and jowls, each a perfect replica of her jawline. It was quite alarming, but the worst of it was her eyes. They looked trapped, like a wild animal trying to get out. Was she burning out too, or was there something else haunting her?

I looked down at the picnic bench and back up at Stacey and wondered how on earth she was going to fit. But she had it well in hand. She placed her tray at the end of the table nearest me, went over and took a chair among many lining the wall of the room, and pushed it over to our table.

She nodded at us all and the rolls of fat around her face jiggled as she sat down beside me. She was not carrying her cane and when, much to my embarrassment, she saw me looking at her bad leg she said, "Just a little sprain." I glanced up at her face then, but she looked away and began fiddling with her food.

"Welcome to Spaniel Island," she said, and unexpectedly she turned and smiled at me. All the fat lines that had dragged down her face suddenly accentuated the loveliness of her smile, which was contagious. Every negative thing I had thought about her was wiped away by that one small smile. Maybe burn out, but not burned out yet.

I smiled back. How could I not?

"Darcy has reminded me that you need some equipment for your experiments."

I nodded.

"I'll get you set up after breakfast." She picked at a plate of food that looked as though it was on a diet itself — a few pieces of dry toast, a glass of skim milk, and a couple of apple slices. More than Melanie but not a lot.

Martha couldn't stand the silence that descended. "So, you're a botanist, right?" she said to Stacey, who swivelled her eyes over to meet Martha's.

"Yes and no." She sat back on her chair. "I'm doing dune succession studies. Looking at how naked dunes become colonized by plants, animals, and insects over time."

Martha's mouth dropped open. "But that would take years."

Stacey smiled again. "Fifteen good ones and counting."

"Are you here every summer?" I asked.

"Every summer. I live in Halifax and got involved in succession when I spent a summer on Sable Island studying their wild horse population for my thesis. It kind of grabbed me how the dunes grow."

"Halifax, eh? A fellow Canadian," I said. Why is it always so nice to meet one of your own when you're away from home?

She nodded.

"Dalhousie?"

"Yeah, for my undergrad, and then McGill."

"But Halifax pulled you back?"

"Halifax has a habit of doing that. And Dalhousie offered me the best job in the best city in Canada. How could I refuse?"

I smiled. Pride of city comes a close second to pride of country. Or maybe they are both in first place, just different versions of the same pride.

"I have to do turtle patrol tonight. Would you like to come?" Stacey asked me.

"Turtle patrol?"

"We patrol the beach every night looking for female sea turtles laying their eggs. Ten o'clock in the clearing?"

I nodded and said thank you, wondering if she was well enough to go on turtle patrol, and then didn't know what else to say so I looked over at Sam and Melanie for relief. He was talking to her about something interesting, his face animated and his hands illustrating whatever he was saying. Melanie was paying rapt attention. Stacey reached over and touched Sam's arm. He stopped in mid-sentence and looked over at Stacey. He hesitated a fraction of a second before he smiled.

"Stop by my office before lunch," she said. "I want that diagram." She dropped her hand then and he nodded, but his mind was definitely elsewhere.

"Dr. Stacey Franklin!"

Stacey froze, toast halfway to her mouth. He had come up behind her and she had to twist to see him, which was difficult for her. Wyatt was dressed in white pants and an indigo rugby shirt that made his blue eyes leap off his face. It somehow seemed criminal for anyone to be as handsome as this guy was.

He'd walked around Stacey's chair and was holding

out his hand.

"We didn't properly meet last night," he said. Stacey tried to get up, a look of sheer frustration on her face. But Wyatt planted his hand on her shoulder to keep her in place while waiting for her to offer her hand. She looked unsure of herself, as if she felt at a disadvantage, or maybe it was just my imagination because she suddenly reached out her hand and gripped his hard.

"A belated welcome to the Spaniel Island Research Station, Dr. Sinclair." I was struck by how much Stacey had notched down the temperature of her voice. It was too strong and too hard and the emphasis on the last name was just plain weird, unless she was nervous for some reason. His good looks must make many a woman do stupid things.

"Call me Wyatt, please. And I trust you are over the flu?" he said and included us all in his invitation, as if we all wanted to call him Wyatt and had all had the flu. Stacey rallied her manners and introduced us all, but instead of sitting down to join us he remained standing by Stacey's right arm.

"I got your note. We need to talk," he said matter-of-factly. She looked at him then with such a vacant look that I thought she couldn't possibly have heard him.

But I was wrong. She looked up at him and smiled a cold, thin smile. "About what? The vaccine?"

He looked discomfited, as if she had said something rude. It appeared the tables had turned and she had the upper hand now, although it was not at all clear why.

"As you must understand, Wyatt, I want to keep things as quiet as possible for the sake of the station. Are you absolutely sure there has been a theft?" She stared at him unblinking and he stared back. "Darcy intimated that you have a reputation for being absentminded. Perhaps you have just misplaced the vaccine? It was just one vial after all."

He stared at her without moving, the two of them like two rams in rut facing off against each other. Stacey won. He backed off, but before he left he said, "Sometimes things aren't as you see them."

"And sometimes they are," she replied.

chapter six

Stacey pushed back her chair and rose slowly to her feet, her plate still full of food.

"I'll send Darcy to show you the equipment," she said to me, and then she was gone.

"Is she always so abrupt?" I asked as I looked over at Sam and Melanie.

"She's got a heart of gold," said Sam "She just doesn't know how to show it."

"She means well," said Melanie.

"Some people find it uncomfortable to be around a weight-challenged person," said Sam, "and she feels that, that she is being judged by her weight and not her mind. It's given her a bit of a chip on her shoulder."

I looked at Melanie, whose face was neutral, and at Martha, whose face was screaming sympathy from every overweight pore.

We had just finished our breakfast when Darcy appeared at our table, his iPod dangling out of one pocket and his iPhone in his hand.

"Latest news — hot off my iPhone," he said. "I've been making the rounds warning everyone. There's a hurricane coming and we are right in its path. If it holds to course we will have to evacuate within forty-eight to sixty hours. If it veers north we'll be okay, but the mainland will get the worst of it."

Martha and I glanced at each other in alarm and she said, "But we just got here."

"Maybe you should have checked the weather forecast," he said, but when I looked at him he was smiling.

"Are they evacuating the mainland?" I asked.

"Not yet, no."

"Surely we're not that much different?" I really did not want to get back in that boat so soon, especially if the seas were swelling.

"It's a barrier island. It got that name for a reason. It can take quite a punch from any hurricane that hits it."

"But we have several rows of pretty impressive dunes between us and the sea," said Martha, who was fiddling with her orange juice, swirling it round and round just like the sea in a storm. I dragged my eyes away from it and back onto Darcy.

"Thing is, Spaniel Island is barely above sea level and a bad hurricane or a direct hit could flood it badly. Those dunes can't hold back the power of a really ugly sea. The barrier islands are always being evacuated, just in case. So please prepare a bag and be ready at short notice." Darcy paused to catch his breath.

Martha's eyes had widened to the size of saucers and the fact that she made no comment was a comment in itself.

"No worries," said Darcy. Martha looked dubious. "It'll probably miss us entirely. Meanwhile — business as usual. I have to go and help Trevor board up some windows but I'll take you to your equipment now if you want." Martha and I collected our dishes, said good-bye to Sam and Melanie, and deposited our trays in the kitchen. Darcy led us out a side door, which led onto the wraparound verandah. We were on the dune side of the building, among the trees, and it was quite dark. The sun had trouble penetrating the canopy. Martha excused herself, saying she had something to do, and I followed Darcy across a wooden bridge to a larger two-storey building. I was amazed that I had not noticed it from the clearing, until I realized it was hidden from view by the turning of the dunes, as the two main buildings followed the curving dune line. It was the exact opposite to the other building, made as it was from cinder blocks three stories tall. It looked like exactly what it was: a research station, with a nod to aesthetics in the vinyl siding that covered most of the cinder blocks. When we entered the new building we entered the universal world of a biology station, from the faint whiff of animal feces to the sickly scent of formaldehyde.

Darcy led me down a pale yellow corridor, lined with prints of cheetah and lions, gazelles and eagles. On each side of the corridor were doors that opened into lab space. Darcy disappeared through the last door on the left and I followed him into a room that was at once familiar and strange. Familiar because it contained the apparatus and equipment of biologists everywhere, from the live traps and mist nets to the radio transmitters and antennas to the binoculars, telescopes, raingear, and hip waders.

Strange, because I'd never been here before, despite the familiarity. Darcy pulled out a parabola and handed it to me. It looked like a giant soup bowl and it helped to concentrate and amplify sound and funnel it into a recorder.

"How long have you been Stacey's assistant?" I asked, and at once realized that it sounded rather abrupt. But he didn't seem to mind.

"'Bout two years. I was her student and she offered me the job. I thought it would be a lark."

"And has it?"

He grinned at me. "You bet. Beats a sit-down job any day." I laughed. I couldn't imagine him sitting down for long.

"Do you think we'll have to evacuate?" I asked.

"That will be Stacey's decision, but it's not looking good. Just one more worry on her back."

"Obviously I don't know her," I said, "but she seems kind of stretched out."

"Yeah, well she's had some kind of stomach flu or something and has been under the weather for the last five days, so she hasn't been about much."

He swivelled his head to look at me, a little dimple in his left cheek twitching.

"Is that why she hadn't met Wyatt?" I asked.

Something in Darcy's face vied for control but lost, and he rearranged his face into a look of pure neutrality. Intrigued, I waited.

"You could say that," he finally said.

Darcy hauled out all my equipment and the two of us spent some time making sure it was working properly. I felt that little twinge of excitement I always get just before I go out into the field. Research is so stimulating because you are testing the unknown to see if your theory works or doesn't work. The collection of raw data is exciting. Photographers know the feeling. The summer I stumbled across a body in the wilderness my brother Ryan had been so transported by his craft that he hadn't noticed the lime green insect he was photographing was perched on a dead man's body. You take your photos, hundreds of them, and then you go through them and find the gems. Only in my case it was getting the birdsong recordings back to the lab, to a machine that would turn the song into symbols on a page. These would then be analyzed to determine if my theory was supported by the data. It was like getting something for free — taking it from nature without leaving a trace — and using it as a palette for my research. I could do field work forever.

Darcy broke into my thoughts and led me back down the long corridor, every door open to the labs beyond. When I commented about it to Darcy he said, "Nobody locks anything around here. That's why the missing vial of vaccine is such a concern. We work on an honour system and have never had any problems until now. And Wyatt isn't helping much — he's being pretty vague about what vial and when. It can't possibly affect his work any, he has extra vaccine, so I guess Stacey's doing damage control for the theft itself, if it is a theft." He paused. "I wish she'd let me do the investigating — she's so weak after the flu — but she'd have none of it when I suggested it."

As we passed one of the labs a voice called out, "Darce?"

Darcy stopped and walked through the open door. I followed behind. Sam was standing amid a bunch of esoteric looking machinery, test tubes, and vials of all descriptions. He handed Darcy a sealed envelope and said, "Would you mind taking that to Stacey, please? It's the diagram she wanted. And she wants it yesterday."

Darcy took the envelope and turned to look at me. "Sam here is our resident forensics man when he isn't batman." I think I was supposed to laugh at that last reference, but Sam rolled up his eyes and I figured he'd heard the joke a million times. Darcy slapped the envelope in his hand and said, "Anything interesting?"

Sam shook his head, but there was a glint in his eye as he said, "Only to Stacey." He smiled then and turned to me and said, "I'll be mist netting some bats tonight. If you see Martha would you ask her if she'd like to come? You are welcome too, of course, seeing as how you were unlucky this morning."

"Does Stacey often ask you to do forensics?" I asked, ignoring his invitation in the haste to get my question out. He was momentarily disconcerted and said no, drawing it out like pull taffy. It was an invitation to elaborate on why I had asked in the first place. Since I wasn't really sure why, I changed the subject back to mist netting and begged off Sam's invitation, citing Stacey's invitation.

As Sam turned back to his work I said, "Is there a map of everyone's study sites so I don't traipse through them?"

Sam smiled. "Ah, you've been talking to Stacey, I see."

I didn't say anything. He and Darcy took me down the hall and into what had to be the biologists' den, their hangout — big fluffy sofas, recliners, and a large TV set, all surrounded by windows looking out over the forest of live oak. The map was pinned on the wall and showed the island in great detail. What struck me most was just how small the island was and how big the neighbouring island, to which it was almost adjoined, was. Everybody's study site was on the map. It was meticulously done and easy to see at a glance where everybody was.

Darcy said, "You'll be mostly up at the north end of the island, the interior parts. The south end is mostly impenetrable." He whisked a sheet of acetate off a nearby desk and laid it over the map at the north end. He used green putty to secure it and then took a black marker and outlined my study site, just like that, even going so far as to pinpoint where he had seen some actual male Indigo Buntings singing. I was itching to get started right away, but it was still way too hot for the birds to be singing their courting songs with any kind of gusto.

I left Darcy and Sam and went back to the cabin to double check the equipment and get all my gear ready. It was such a heady feeling! When I was satisfied that everything was working I took a tour around the clearing. Basically it was a network of paths through the palmetto and live oak, meandering from the various cabins and widening into a sandy area the size of a four-car garage, mostly covered in live oak leaves, at the base of the stairs to the mess. Five or six ATVs were parked near the stairs and someone was tinkering with one of them. There was a lot of cursing going on and I sauntered over to see what was happening. The man with the shaggy beard, Trevor, who had piloted our boat, was sitting knee-deep in tools and bits of vehicle. He looked up and caught my eye, his scowl slowly softening. "These damn machines are so temperamental. They are always and perpetually sick, which makes me sick." He looked sick too — his moth-eaten beard partially hid a sallow complexion and sunken eyes that screamed out at me, but I wasn't sure what they were trying to say.

I looked at the array of vehicles and asked him if I would be able to use one of them to get to my study site — which was quite far up the island.

"Stacey didn't tell you which one you could use?" He spat out Stacey's name as if he was getting rid of something unpalatable.

I shook my head.

"That one over there — the red three wheeler. It's all yours. Key's in the ignition, gas tank is full. Just hold the throttle and she'll be fine. But be kind to her. She's really old." I hadn't heard of a three wheeler in years and wasn't even sure if they were still legal. I decided not to ask.

"Are you a mechanic?" I asked instead, looking at all his tools.

"Hah! Me, a mechanic? Only by happenstance." He scowled. "No one else around here can fix these hunks of junk."

"Don't let him fool you." The voice came from behind me, and we both turned. She stood there like a model, totally at ease with every part of her body, her beauty more related to how she held herself and the confidence she exuded than anything else. What do they say when a woman has "it," that something you cannot learn. Well, this woman had it in spades.

"He's really a very good mechanic," she said, but there was a hard edge to her tone as she offered her hand to me. Her luxuriant, jet-black, curly hair shone in the sun as it cascaded down around her shoulders and her mahogany eyes had such depth of colour that they were mesmerizing. "I'm Jayne. Who might you be?"

I took her hand and introduced myself. Jayne turned back to the bearded man and said, "Trevor's our Jack of all trades. When he's not a mechanic he captains our ferries, when he's not captaining our ferries he's captaining a shrimp boat, and when he's not doing that he's the local taxi on the island. Isn't that right, Trevor?" Did I detect a note of sarcasm in her voice?

Trevor scowled again and returned to his work as Jayne bent down and picked up some luggage from a pile dumped behind one of the ATVs. She was more than happy to accept when I offered to help and she led me down one of the palmetto-invested trails to a cabin that looked just like mine. Except it appeared that Jayne had it all to herself.

"Trevor scowls rather a lot," I said by way of conversation, realizing too late that it sounded like a rather leading question.

"Only around me," she said, and then added, "and Stacey, of course." I didn't see any "of course" about it and he'd scowled at me and I said so.

She smiled. "It'll take you awhile to get the hang of the place," was all she said. I changed topics as I helped her carry her luggage into the cabin.

"You're the turtle lady."

She laughed. "My pictures give me away?" she asked and flung her arm to take in dozens of pictures of sea turtles gracing every inch of her walls.

I laughed in return.

"I've been studying turtles of one kind or another since I was a little girl. They fascinate me. They are so ancient and have survived for millions of years. They swam the same seas as the dinosaurs. We can't even come close to saying that about ourselves, and yet here we are endangering sea turtles for the sake of a shrimp cocktail or a bowl of soup. It's criminal but the courts don't seem to really know that yet."

She paused and threw me a small metal ring with a removable rubber cap. I turned it over in my hand, trying to figure out what it was. I looked up at her and shrugged. She smiled and took the ring and cap from me and pulled the cap off. The brass ring was quite a bit smaller than a dime and the rubber cap was essentially another ring slightly smaller with a hunk of black rubber glued to it. She held up the ring and said, "I've done quite a few experiments over the years on the visual orientation of sea turtle hatchlings. It is quite extraordinary that the hatchlings, the size of a plum but flatter, come up out of a dark nest into a dark night and yet they make their way unerringly to the sea." She took the ring back from me. "It's really cool. I mean how do they manage to find the sea when they are so tiny that one dune is like Everest to them? At their level, which is about half an inch above the ground, they can't even see the sea. The literature has pretty much confirmed that they are programmed to head toward the brightest horizon. But how are they programmed and when does the switch turn on and turn off — because it has to turn off or sea turtles would never come ashore to lay their eggs, they would always be swimming toward the brightest horizon, which is out to sea."

She picked up a little rubber sea turtle hatchling from her bedside table and fitted the brass ring over one of its eyes.

"They're goggles," she said. "I glue the brass ring over the eye and then I can use the cap to blind one eye or both or change the rubber for colour filters."

I tried not to laugh but I couldn't help smiling. The image it conjured up in my mind was hilarious.

"I know," she said. "Everybody laughs. It is funny and they do look ludicrous when they are wearing them, but it is harmless to the turtles. The glue peels off and I release them to the sea after any experiments. You wouldn't believe how many people want to interview me about my bespectacled turtles. They are much more interested in that than in my nest predation studies."

I rose to the bait. "Which are?"

"Oh, you know. I check each nest in our little hatchery here after it has come up and analyze the contents for diseased or depredated eggs, et cetera."

"You have a hatchery on the island?" I asked, surprised and not all that interested in the contents of an old nest. I hadn't read anything about the hatchery and no one had mentioned it.

"Well, it's really a tiny hatchery. Most of the nests laid by the females we leave in place now, but it used to be that every nest that was laid was dug up and transferred to a fenced-in area so that the feral pigs and other animals didn't gorge themselves. Now we only dig up a few nests for research purposes. We get the odd photographer too who wants to film a nest erupting. It's quite a sight. You should sit up one night — they only come up at night — and see if you get lucky."

"So you did your Ph.D. on sea turtles?"

She grunted.

"Where did you do it? What university?"

She moved suddenly and tripped over a pair of shoes on the floor. After I made the motions of helping her up I tried to take up where we left off, but she was having none of it. The moment was lost.

chapter seven

During lunch we all listened to the radio and news of Hurricane Chase. It had pummelled the DR and Haiti and was barrelling down on the eastern seaboard of the United States — touchdown estimated at Charleston, South Carolina. We were right in its path unless some unforeseen phenomenon steered it away. As a result we were on alert for evacuation within twenty-four hours. It was frustrating, exciting, and a bit frightening, all at the same time. Now that I had seen the island and realized we were really only as high above sea level as the mercurial dunes that formed the island, it kind of hit home what sitting ducks we were. But nobody seemed too perturbed about it so I assumed everything was under control.

Darcy and Trevor had boarded up all the windows in the mess and it was even more gloomy and oppressive in there now. After lunch, in the energy-draining heat of early afternoon, everyone disappeared or hung around in the lounge listening to news about the hurricane, reading books, or catching up on research. I chose the siesta in an effort to catch up on the sleep that Martha had stolen from me. I awoke in that nasty grogginess that seems to happen when you sleep out of turn. It was still drenchingly hot and I felt like a pancake, flat and sizzling. I looked at the clock on my bedside table. It was time to go in search of some buntings. I wondered where Martha was as I got my equipment together. I stuffed the recording paraphernalia into my packsack, hefted the parabola in my hands, and went off in search of my trusty steed. As Trevor had promised it was an old three-wheeler — an anachronism actually since three wheelers are no longer sold because they're so tippy. I'd never ridden one before but I figured it couldn't be much different from a motorcycle. There was no rack to put my parabola on, so I had to put it on my lap. She started like a dream but she stuttered and jerked as I backed her up. I was glad no one was watching as I finally got her turned around while gripping the parabola with my knees. It was awkward and I finally had to drive one-handed down the leaf-laden track to the island's main artery — a wider leaf-laden track. I had the map in my pocket and a compass but I was pretty sure I knew where I was going, having studied the map earlier. Except when I got to the main line everything looked the same — a long tunnel through the oaks with many narrower tracks branching off. There were some quaint signs along the way and with their help I made it to the north end of the island where the forest thinned out, as if it had once been logged, and the territory began to look more like Indigo Bunting territory: open with good perching trees nearby. But it wasn't big, and I began to worry about getting enough study subjects. I parked my three wheeler, got my equipment set up, earphones on, the electronic recorder slung over my left shoulder, the parabola hooked up to the electronic recorder and perched in my right hand. I took a GPS reading and moved down the trail slowly, listening to the birdsong of painted buntings, sparrows, hawks, and more. But no indigos. After half an hour of walking and stopping to listen I was starting to get discouraged. I had to wonder how all those biologists could sit in blinds for hours and hours. What was half an hour to that? And then I heard him, the lively, clear, complex notes of an Indigo Bunting. I turned on my recording gear and taped a bunch of his songs while I scanned the foliage to try and locate him, to see that beautiful brilliant indigo blue of his feathers. But he proved elusive. I took a GPS reading and walked on out of the range of the first little bunting, looking for a second.

Two hours later I had two male buntings recorded, which I considered a good day's work. But I was thoroughly lost. I'd parked my three wheeler on the main road but had somehow found my way onto a secondary road. I took out my GPS and started heading back when the trail I was on broke into a clearing with a sign that said LIGHTHOUSE ROAD and I could see the beach in the distance, behind the line of dunes. I looked at my watch. Still lots of time before the sun set, so I stashed all my equipment under a lofty live oak and made my way out into the dunes. The sun had lost its heat but the air was still and thick. When I meandered my way among the ten-foot dunes I saw a line of orange stakes circling several of the dunes that had some vegetation on them. I figured they had to be Stacey's dunes and I looked at them with some interest. *How old were they?* I wondered. Surely the life span of a dune on a barrier island had to be fleeting — unless of course vegetation took hold, as they had on these ones — they needed something to slow or stop the effects of the wind, which otherwise kept them in constant motion. I made a point of walking in the valleys of the dunes when I could, to keep my environmental footprint tiny — nothing quite as invasive as skidding down the face of a dune, bringing a cascade of sand with you. As I began to break out onto the beach above the high-tide line I could see the swells of the sea cresting over the shallow waters and crashing onto the beach. The water looked grey, leaden, greasy, as if it was gearing up for something — was this what a hurricane sea looked like in the days before the hurricane hit? There weren't any shells on the beach as I headed toward the south end of the island, but I could see the tidal creek that separated Spaniel Island from its much bigger neighbour. It looked pretty benign — no sign of the current that had carried the spaniel and the little boy out to the sandbar. But then again the tide was coming in.

I climbed the beach and found a nice spot to take a rest among the dunes. But after ten minutes I grew restless and got out my binoculars to survey what I could see of the beach. I jerked the binoculars back when movement caught my eye and watched as one, two, and then three horses moved into view from behind a dune, their tails flicking at the wind and their heads down, snuffling the vegetation at high tide mark. Wild horses conjure images of magnificent stallions with gleaming black coats, heads thrown back, reading the wind. These horses were more like ponies with dull coats and little pot bellies. The two other horses joined the first one and the three of them stood in a tableau of indecision, standing on the threshold of flight. And then I heard a soft *thwip* sound and one of the horses took off, followed immediately by the other two. I watched, mesmerized, as Wyatt and Rosemary appeared from behind a dune, a modified rifle still clutched in Wyatt's hand. Rosemary looked up then and saw me and I heard my name riding the wind that had crept up. She waved at me even as Wyatt made an impatient gesture with his hand. Did I go and join them at Rosemary's invitation or leave at Wyatt's? What the hell. I wanted to watch their operation so I walked down the beach.

By the time I got there the horses were long gone. Wyatt hefted the rifle over his shoulder and I said, "Is that how you do it? You just shoot the vaccine into the horse?"

"It's a dart," he said impatiently. "You dart the animal and the dart injects the vaccine and no more little foals." He laughed. "One down, one to go," he said as he patted the rifle.

"There are only two mares on the entire island?" I asked incredulously. I had just assumed that these three horses were a breakaway pod from the main herd.

"Yup. Seems a bit like overkill doesn't it?"

Was it my imagination or was there a tinge of derision in those words?

I left Wyatt and Rosemary and meandered my way back through the dunes toward my equipment and then to my trike. I turned one last time to look at the sea and saw a man, his back to me, looking out across the vast expanse of ocean. There was something about him that seemed familiar. I grappled for my binoculars, brought them up to my eyes, and scanned the beach looking for him. He leapt into the centre of my lenses, suddenly far bigger than he had been, and I smiled. Duncan. He had said he was going to come down while we were here but he had been very vague about when. He had turned and was starting to walk away down the beach so I ran and yelled into the wind, the sand clawing at my feet and making the going slow. Finally my voice must have pierced through the wind and I watched him stop and then turn to face me. When I drew alongside him in the swirling wind the sun was shining in my eyes and I had to bring my hand up as a guard to see his face clearly, so he beat me to it and gave me a big bear hug. I was in danger of suffocating before he let me go, saying "Pretty nice, eh?"

I looked at the blond windswept beach and the flock of pelicans just skimming the water so that one little riffle of the wind might touch their wings and send them cartwheeling through the surf, and I looked at the sea, still resolutely determined not to let the sun make it shine, and I nodded. There really wasn't anything I could say that could describe it.

"Well, my dear girl, I've seen that look before."

I looked at him quizzically.

"It means you're stricken, afflicted, besotted, bedeviled, smitten, enamoured, moonstruck, captivated, gaga ..." and he waved his hand to encompass the island.

"Don't worry," he added. "It's a common affliction."

"And the antidote is?"

"Why, to buy a place on the island, of course." He chuckled.

"And get involved in island politics?"

"That, I admit, is not idyllic, but it is worth the price." Duncan turned and started walking down the beach. I followed.

"What do you know about this vaccination fiasco?" I asked as I caught up to him.

"Good word for it. It heated up into a really messy situation with both sides trying to strong-arm the membership to vote their way." Duncan stooped and picked up a small moon shell that had been rubbed raw and left dull and lifeless by the sand. He pocketed it. *To each to their own*, I thought.

"It was pretty ugly, actually," he continued. "A lot of strong words, best left unsaid, have been said. It's split the membership in two."

"But it's just two mares and a stallion," I said, trying not to sound too astounded.

"C'mon, Cordi. You're the zoologist. These horses have only just arrived here from the other island. The herd grows one foal at a time. One mare at a time. Eventually the herd will be big enough to harm the island because of the horses' grazing."

"I take it you're for the vaccination?"

"Damn right. How could you think otherwise? But it's caused a lot of bad blood and people are pretty fired up over it. Not sure how it's going to end, but I hope sanity prevails."

We walked along the beach for a little while, the wet sand dark and glistening against the dazzling white of the dry sand. The wind had picked up considerably and we were having a hard time hearing each other. Duncan pointed off to my left and yelled in my ear. "My cabin is just behind the third dune on the left — if you come by the main road it's the first left after Hunter's — you and Martha will have to come for supper one night."

I yelled back into his ear — I had to stand on tiptoes to reach it — "We may have been evacuated by then."

Duncan laughed and waved his hand dismissively. I didn't catch what he said.

"You mean we won't be evacuated?" I guessed.

He shook his head again. "No, I mean I won't be evacuated."

"You mean the authorities won't evacuate you for some reason or you won't evacuate when ordered."

"The latter," he said it as if it made eminent sense.

"But the island could be annihilated. It is a barrier island after all."

He laughed again. "I've been under evacuation orders five times since I bought my cabin and not once have I left." He sounded proud of it.

I was about to say "isn't that stupid?" but caught myself in time. Instead I said, "Do you think that is a wise idea?"

He chose to pretend he didn't hear and shortly after that we parted ways and I headed back toward my trike. I had to use the GPS because all the dunes looked the same. I found the trail out to the beach where I had stowed my stuff and headed down it to find my trike, amazed at how the oaks and the dunes and the palmetto silenced the sounds of the sea and blocked the sun. The sun was low in the sky and my growling stomach made me wonder what happened if you missed dinner at the station. Most biology stations had a system for latecomers — they had to. Biologists are notorious for queer working hours — you had to work the shifts of the animals you were studying, day or night. At any given time at a research station a handful of researchers would sleep through the day, their clocks at odds with everyone else.

I was hot, dirty, sweaty, and tired when I got back to the cabin. Martha had set up her printer on my bed and had printed out a slew of photos. A lot of them were taken last night and were remarkably clear, although the green tinge from the night-vision technology was unfortunate. The screen door screeched open and in she walked, carrying a humungous sandwich and a can of pop, both of which she handed to me.

"Latecomers' leftovers," she said. "How did it go?"

"Two buntings." I patted the recorder.

"Sure they're both buntings?" She was never going to let me live down my colossal mistake when I first started recording birds. I had recorded fifteen individual birds over a week, but when I got the recordings back to the lab and printed out the sonograms it turned out that half the birds were of a different species entirely from the one I was supposed to be studying. In my defence, I never claimed I had a good ear.

I waved my arm at her photos to change the subject. "I see you got some pictures last night."

"It's actually a video, but you can take stills from it."

She picked up one of the photos of a blurry little blob that looked like an owl in a tree and said, "I have to try and get a better picture of this little guy. My hand must have jerked." She sighed and dropped the photo back on my bed, the one I wanted to go to sleep on. "Don't worry, Cordi. When you need me I'll be around." It took me a minute to realize what she was saying.

It sounded vaguely accusatory and I rose to my own defence. "I'll be needing you for some of the analysis, but the field work is solitary. You know that, Martha." Martha was an inveterate talker and the only time I had ever taken her with me to record birds she hadn't been able to keep quiet, and keeping quiet is an essential tool in a biologist's arsenal.

"I'll get you sonograms of these two birds then. There's a machine in the lab." She still sounded hurt but there was nothing I could do about it.

"They have a sonogram machine? That would be great. By the way, Stacey is taking me out turtling tonight. Would you like to come?" My little salvo of reconciliation.

She hesitated. "Sam is going to take me batting tonight. He's doing a quick and dirty experiment. We're going to mist net ten bats and fit them with tiny capsules full of phosphorescent and let them go." Martha's face was lighting up like the phosphorescent capsules and I marvelled at how fast she could change and at Sam's total failure to communicate to me what sounded like a great research project. All he had said was that he was going mist netting. Anyway, I'd accepted Stacey's invitation.

"Everyone will be stationed near a place called Hunter's," she said, oblivious to my envy, "with walkie-talkies, and we'll call in our observations on where the bats are, if they're flying high or low, east or west. If you don't go turtling you should come with us."

No one can ever say that biology isn't interesting, even amusing sometimes. I had pictures of phosphorescent bats zooming around at canopy level, below canopy level, palmetto level, and every level in between, with people hidden at strategic places spying on them. Were biologists the animal kingdom's version of a private eye?

I watched Martha cleaning up the photos from my bed. When she was finished I sat down and said, "You'll never guess who I saw on the beach."

"Duncan," she said, without hesitation. Not even a little bit to make me think she didn't know. No surprises for Martha.

"He dropped by here while you were out birding. The only person coming to the island when everyone else is leaving."

"He told me that if an evacuation order came down he would not be leaving."

Martha chuckled. "Stubborn old bastard."

"I could think of a better word."

"Yeah, he's probably a little bit crazy too, but he told me his cabin is on the highest ground on the island next to the lighthouse."

"The lighthouse?" I remembered the sign I had seen when I was taping birds and wondered how close I had been to it.

"You haven't seen the lighthouse? You've got to be kidding me. It's huge and the tallest thing by far on the island. You can see it for miles. How did you miss it?"

"I guess I wasn't looking the right way."

"I climbed to the very top today and you can see the whole beach and the next island over too. There's even a catwalk at the top, but it looked kind of dicey."

By the time Martha had packed herself up in preparation for batting she looked like a walking advertisement for MEC. She was wearing long crimson pants tucked into her white socks and a long-sleeved green button-down shirt with every button buttoned up. In final preparation she took out a bottle of bug dope and rubbed it on her face, neck, and hands. Then she fastened a bandana on her head and covered it with a big mosquito and no-see-um-proof bug hat. By the time she left I had more or less fallen asleep and awoke with a start five minutes from being late for my 10:00 meeting with Stacey.

The wind was pretty impressive. Even in the shelter of the dunes the great oaks were thrashing and writhing about when I left my cabin and walked into the clearing. Stacey was leaning over a four wheeler equipped with an open cargo area at the back, parked under the one light illuminating the clearing. She acknowledged me with a grunt. She was futzing around with some of the guts of the vehicle, but her great girth was giving her trouble. Biologists the world over have to become good at jury-rigging various pieces of mechanical and electrical equipment. Either that or see their research stall for lack of an electrician or a mechanic in the far flung parts of the earth where they find themselves.

Stacey finally finished what she was doing and sat down behind the handlebars, but she took up the entire seat and I had to ride in the trunk at the back.

The night was overcast, and the forest was inky dark. We bounced and jangled down through the tunnel of trees and around a corner into the blinding glare of headlights. They seemed to have come from nowhere. Stacey swore and swerved the bike viciously to the right. A half-ton truck went left in a spray of sand and grinding gears.

We'd barely come to a standstill when Stacey started yelling. "You idiot," she shouted, as Trevor opened the door of the truck, jammed a baseball cap on his head, and stepped out.

"Why the hell were you going so fast? You could have killed us. Or was that the intent?" Trevor smiled that sickly sort of smile that signals contempt, derision, and agreement, which made me wonder why he might want to kill us, or rather, Stacey.

"No harm done, now is there?" he said slowly.

Stacey glared at him and he touched his cap at her and turned back to his car. "Sayonara," he said, but his smile said something else.

chapter eight

We didn't talk on the way out to the beach. I think we were both pretty riled up, or at least I was. Besides, yelling in her ear was not an attractive option. When we broke out of the forest into the first row of dunes the sky was seething with clouds and the sea's swells were giving way to waves crashing upon the shoreline, the broken bits a startling white in contrast to the monochromatic swells.

Stacey leaned over and yelled above the wind and the waves. "Unlikely to find any females in this weather," she said, and I found I was really disappointed. I had never seen a sea turtle lay eggs. I had never seen a sea turtle period, except on TV. The drill was to drive the full six-kilometre length of the beach once an hour until dawn, searching for females who only laid their eggs at night. The turtle patrol did this every night, dusk to dawn, during nesting season from May to August. Stacey, it seemed, was filling in for a few days while the guys who usually did it went to a wedding on the mainland.

I wondered why she couldn't have found someone else, since she didn't seem to have recovered from her flu bug yet and she was director, after all. But then maybe she was like so many biologists the world over — just powering through their own adversities for the sake of the research.

It only took us half an hour to make the drive, so we had a fifteen-minute break at each end before setting out again.

There were no no-see-ums in this weather — it was way too windy — so we pulled over for one of our breaks and she brought out a thermos and a couple of hunks of bread and cheese and offered me some.

"I love this job and I hate it," she said, to the cascade of stars overhead and to me, it would seem, though why she felt the need to tell me I didn't know. I looked up. The stars were trying valiantly to poke through the massing clouds and the wind was whipping sand in our faces.

I looked at her and she sighed.

"Oh, I don't always like turtle patrol. It can get pretty monotonous, but I don't have to do it very often. What I love is identifying a problem that needs to be solved and figuring out how to solve it. There's nothing like the thrill of research. It's got everything, mystery, intrigue, challenge, even fear and the adrenaline rush you get when your data supports your theory or when you see a sea turtle nesting for the first time."

I couldn't have said it better, even though I'd often tried. I took a swig from the thermos and handed it back to her. "You've been director for five years?"

My bald question put paid to our shared moment of camaraderie and she had a guarded look on her face as she said, "Yes."

When she didn't follow it up with anything I said, "You said you hate the job too."

"Everyone hates a part of their jobs. It's human nature," she said evasively. But she seemed sad and at the same time angry. She went quiet then and took the thermos and swabbed it down with the towel before packing it away.

"Sorry we haven't found a nesting turtle for you. Next time." She turned on the bike and the engine roared to life.

I looked at my watch. It was only 10:45 and she had told me that the turtle patrol went until dawn. She noticed me looking at my watch and said, "I don't like the look of the weather. If we are going to evacuate the island it will be at dawn. I need to get back in time in case there is an alert." She patted her walkie-talkie and said, "These don't always work."

At first I thought it was a huge boulder in the distance, sitting on the edge of the sea, but then it moved. I squeezed Stacey's shoulder, but she had already seen it. We drove up off the beach and Stacey shut off the vehicle's lights.

"Light will scare her back into the surf," she said as we sat and waited. The sea turtle was about the size of a truck's tire and she emerged from the sea with all the grace of a ponderous tank. Like an invalid she hauled herself painfully (or at least painful to watch) up the beach, each movement of her front flippers plowing through the sand making her whole body shudder. She left a trail of flipper marks behind her, each mark nearly touching the one in front. Like walking heel to toe. A completely graceless animal on land and yet in the sea she was as graceful as a soaring bird. She finally stopped above the high-tide mark and we could just make out her hind flippers scooping sand and sending it flying as she dug her nest. Stacey turned the bike back on and we drove up close. I was worried we were going to scare her. Any other animal would have turned tail at the ATV bearing down on them.

"Once she starts laying her eggs she is impervious to everything," said Stacey. We sat and watched as she laboriously scooped out a hole the size of a basketball and the shape of a flask. The eggs were white and leathery and looked like ping pong balls, but were about the size of a golf ball and were covered in stringy mucous. I was being anthropomorphic but it seemed as though it was taking a lot out of her — her eyes were welling up with tears and she was breathing erratically. But sea turtles had been doing this for millions of years so it obviously worked. And then it was done and she began filling in the hole with her hind flippers. When she was satisfied she thumped the top of the nest four or five times with her whole body — essentially doing pushups and then letting her body fall. She then threw a lot of sand around to disguise the nest. And then she was gone, making her way back to the sea, leaving a lonely trail of flipper prints behind her to show she had been there. We didn't talk the whole way home. Stacey seemed subdued and I was just plain tired. When we got back the clearing was deserted. "Doesn't look as though anything's happening here," said Stacey in a voice that sounded sorry.

The station was in almost total darkness, except for a nightlight in the main building and a light in the clearing where we stood. The live oaks were being pummelled by the wind overhead and somewhere something was making a rhythmic clanking noise.

"Guess there's no evacuation." We said good night and I headed off to my cabin. Martha wasn't back yet from batting and I couldn't sleep so I was reading when she burst into the cabin about three hours later and said, "I just bumped into Darcy. We're to be evacuated in forty minutes." Since I didn't have much to pack I was ready in five minutes, but Martha couldn't decide what to take in the little bag that Darcy had said each of us could take — valuables only and one change of clothes. We'd already been briefed on where to meet. Trevor was already there and so were Wyatt and Rosemary when we arrived. The others straggled in. Darcy gave us a refresher talk and we loaded into Trevor's van, which sat twelve uncomfortably. I was the last one in and that's when Darcy asked where Stacey was. Nobody said anything and Darcy, who was jammed between two people, looked at me beseechingly and said, "Can you check her cabin please?" I nodded and loped down the path leading to Stacey's cabin.

There was a light on the porch but the cabin was in darkness. I took the two steps in one bound, called her name through the darkened screen door, and stood listening as the wind screamed overhead. It had started to rain again and I could hear it pinging on her metal roof. When she didn't reply I figured she was sleeping and I called louder. When she still didn't respond I opened the door and walked inside. There was a strange sweet smell to the air and I tried to remember if Stacey wore perfume. It was too dark to make out anything but big dark shapes and I fished around for a light. I found it by the door and switched it on. I saw her sitting on a chair with her back to me, her head rolled forward on her chest, sleeping. I called her name again but again there was no response. The thought occurred to me that maybe she was ill. I walked quickly around the chair so I could see her face — and wished I hadn't. Someone had tied her legs to the chair and each of her hands to an arm, but what made me gag was the duct tape silencing her mouth and another strip blocking her nose. I stood there and stared while my mind imagined her horrible end. So lost in her tragedy was I that I didn't hear Darcy until he was beside me.

"Jesus," was all he said. We stood there unable to get out of the moment that imprisoned us. If it hadn't been for the branch of a tree crashing down on the roof we might have stayed there staring at her forever. But it jolted us out of our shock. I grabbed a corner of the duct tape and peeled it from her nose and then did the same with her mouth. Then I leaned forward and felt for a pulse, feeling guilty that I hadn't done so right away. But there was nothing. No telltale throbbing indicating a life was still there.

"Help me get her on the ground," I said. "We may still be able to save her. She's still warm." I saw the hope creep into his face and it gave me some courage.

I started undoing her left wrist, which was rubbed raw by the rope while Darcy took the right. They were tight slip knots and it took some loosening but we got her on the ground and began CPR.

"Cordi, what's wrong? What's happened?" I looked up to see Martha standing dripping in the doorway, her lifejacket deflated around her neck, ready and waiting for a disaster on the trip to the mainland, and her camera dangling from her shoulder. How long had she been there? Long enough to see the duct tape? In that moment she looked so human, so frail, so full of hopes and dreams, just like the life I was trying to save. But Stacey's life had run out. She was gone. It was 3:30 a.m.

Martha had moved into the room and was standing beside me.

"They sent me to find out what was taking you so long," she said, her face betraying the calmness of her voice and the banality of her question in the face of what lay before us.

"What do we do now?" asked Darcy, the hope in his face now supplanted by disbelief and something else I couldn't quite place.

"We evacuate," I said.

"But what about Stacey?"

"Nothing we can do for her now. We'll notify the police as soon as we get to the mainland."

"But she'll, you know, in this heat." His voice stuttered to a halt as he looked down at Stacey, now sprawled on the floor. He looked up and visibly squared his shoulders as he said; "We have to get her up to the walk-in refrigerator in the main building." He looked from me to Martha to Stacey and added, "I'll come with you to the compound and then Trevor and I can come back and get her up."

"But Trevor says it's the last boat out," said Martha.

Darcy looked through her. "I can't just leave her here all alone. It's the least I can do for Stacey. But please don't tell anybody. We'll just say she's like the captain of a sinking ship. She won't leave."

Darcy moved toward the door but Martha stood transfixed and I gently took her by the arm. But she shrugged me off and said, as she unslung her camera, "This is a crime scene, Cordi, and there's no one here to process it. I should take some pictures for the police before Darcy moves the body."

It hadn't even occurred to me what a mess we'd made of this crime scene until Martha said that. "There's no time for that," I said, but she fired off a few shots anyway.

We left then, shutting the screen door and the storm door tightly behind us.

Everyone was packed into the truck like sardines and getting pretty pissed off. Our explanation didn't allay that frustration much. They just turned it on Stacey, saying how selfish she was, and I felt badly that we were letting them make ill of the dead when they didn't know that she was dead. But then again, somebody other than Darcy, Martha, and I knew she was dead. We squeezed into the truck and headed through the forest to the compound. Twice we had to stop and clear branches from the trail, the rain pelting us relentlessly. One of the branches was so big that Trevor had to chainsaw it in two places. It was dark in the woods but as we reached the compound we could see that dawn had come and almost gone. We were an hour late.

We all tumbled out of the truck and followed Trevor up to the wharf. It was hard to see in the rain because the wind was picking up and throwing itself at us horizontally, but it was pretty easy to see that there was no boat at the wharf. *Someone had taken it*, I thought. Trevor waved us over to one of the metal outbuildings. Once we were inside he took out his cellphone and punched in a number. We all huddled around him, waiting. I was amazed that he got through in these conditions. As he clicked his cell shut it was obvious by the glum look on his face that all was not well.

"Some islanders took the boat when we didn't show up. They can't come back for us," he said. "They had a hell of a trip and no one is willing to risk it. We're on our own."

Everybody began talking at once.

"We'll drown if we stay on the island." Rosemary.

"Cool." Sam.

"My snakes!" Melanie.

"Who's going to be in charge?" Darcy.

"God damnit, I've got court cases I can't miss." David.

"Christ. Some working holiday this turned out to be." Wyatt.

"Oh my god. My study site." Jayne.

We were a bedraggled bunch, our clothes soaked through and our hair plastered to our heads, when Trevor got us all back into the truck and we headed back the way we came through the wildly flailing branches of the trees overhead and the torrential rains. The windshield wipers weren't fast enough to put a dent in the rain slamming against the windshield and to the swirling thoughts in my head. I couldn't get the vision of Stacey out of my mind, her face covered in duct tape, her hands tied. Less than five hours before we had watched a sea turtle together on the beach and had connected with each other on some weird level. Who could have done such a thing and why? I looked around at my seatmates, the thought eating into me that one of them could have done it, must have done it. Or maybe one of the islanders did it.

We all made it back in one piece physically — emotionally I wasn't going to hazard a guess. Before we got out of the truck into the deaf-making madness of the storm, Darcy asked us all to meet in the dining room in half an hour to discuss strategy. He then got out of the truck and headed in the direction of Stacey's cabin.

Martha and I made our way to our cabin. The ground was soaked and squishy and was beginning to puddle. There were twigs everywhere and I began to wonder how safe it was to stay here. We hadn't had time to change out of our wet clothes when Darcy knocked on the door and invited himself in. It was a small cabin with three very wet people streaming water onto the floor. All I wanted to do was to get into some dry clothes and I told Darcy as much. But he didn't seem to be listening and I got the feeling he was rehearsing what he wanted to say to us. To me, it turned out.

"Stacey told me a bit about you," he said.

I looked suitably perplexed.

"As director she has certain responsibilities and she had to vet you to make sure you were a bona fide researcher." He laughed through his nose. "She was kind of paranoid about that."

When I didn't respond — how could I? — he continued. "I'm out of my league here. I don't know how to handle Stacey's death — murder, I guess. Normally I'd just call the police and have them handle it but I guess that is out of the question, for the time being anyway." He pushed some wet hair off his cheek. The cabin light flickered.

"You've been involved with at least two murder investigations up in Canada, according to Stacey. I was hoping you could help me out here."

"I don't understand."

"What do I do about Stacey?"

"Call the police," I said, knowing what was coming next.

"I will but they can't come over to the island until the hurricane is over. What do we do? Do we tell everybody or do we keep it a secret?"

I wondered how carrying Stacey up the stairs to the refrigerator could be kept a secret.

"I think we have to tell everyone," I said.

"They know she is here on the island," said Martha, "and I don't think we can keep her death a secret. And why should we?"

"To avoid panic," said Darcy.

"But we don't have to tell people she was murdered," I said.

Before I could say anything more he said, "I would like to ask you if you would tell people what happened and reassure them that everything is okay and to deal with the police."

I started to protest but he raised his hand to stop me. "You have more authority on the subject of murder than any one of us and we need someone like you right now."

How could I say no to that?

chapter nine

"Like a moth to the flame," said Martha, as she struggled out of her wet clothes.

"What are you talking about?" I asked, knowing exactly what she was talking about.

"Murder seems to follow you around."

"You can't always choose your bedfellows," I said. "Or are you trying to make me feel like a hex?" The light flickered again in the cabin and we looked at each other.

"Besides, you helped solve the other murders, so I could say murder follows you around too," I said.

"Yeah, but I never get to find the bodies."

"Lucky you." I laughed. "Do you think Duncan's still on the island?"

"Why?"

"He could be a big help in processing the crime scene."

"Because he's a pathologist?"

"Precisely. He can at least establish time of death for us."

"Are we going to try and solve this?"

"Why not? We have Duncan. We have you as the official photographer. We even have Sam for some simple toxicology if we need it."

"But the police can do all that when they come. They won't like it if you compromise their crime scene."

"It's already been compromised. Besides, they're not the ones cooped up with a murderer." Said that way it made me shudder.

We finished dressing and left the cabin to meet everyone in the dining room. As we struggled up all those stairs in the driving rain I wondered how the hell we were going to get Stacey up there.

We sat down at a table with Sam, Melanie, Wyatt, and Rosemary who were all talking about the failed evacuation and who was to blame. By the number of times Stacey's name came up, she was to blame. She should have ordered the evacuation earlier. Darcy and Jayne arrived together, followed by David. Darcy caught my eye and nodded toward the back of the dining room.

"What do we do about Stacey's brother?" he asked.

"Stacey's brother?" I asked, puzzled.

"Yeah, he can't find out with everyone else. It would be cruel."

"I don't follow. Who is Stacey's brother?"

"You don't know?" He looked at me in surprise. "David. David is Stacey's brother. He's a lawyer from New England." I thought back to the tall thin man hugging the round fat woman and marvelled at how a brother and sister could be so different.

"You have to tell him first, before you tell everyone else." Darcy's voice intruded on my thoughts.

You?

"You mean you have to tell him."

"I can't. He hates my guts. It would be unkind coming from me."

I looked over at David, who had taken a seat beside Jayne.

"I'll run interference with the crowd until you've told him," said Darcy.

I really, really did not want to do this, but Darcy had his hand on my arm and was squeezing it, definitely in supplication, and with a sinking heart I walked over to David and asked him if I could have a private word with him. I led him out into the hallway and down to the lounge. He looked at me expectantly.

"I'm really sorry to have to tell you this, but your sister died this evening."

He was very still, not a flicker of emotion crossed his face. He was like an automaton. The silence lengthened between us and I tried to think of something to say.

"How?" he finally said.

"We won't know that until an autopsy is performed," I lied.

He nodded. "Where is she?"

"In her cabin."

"Is that where it happened?"

I nodded again.

"What are you going to do with her?" he asked in a slow even voice.

"Pardon?" I asked, gathering my thoughts.

"You can't leave her like that, not in this temperature," and he wiped his arm across his sweaty forehead to illustrate his point.

"Darcy has made arrangements to clear out the walk-in fridge. We'll move her up as soon as Duncan has seen her."

"Who the hell is Duncan?"

"He's a pathologist who owns a cabin on the island. He's also a medical examiner."

"Is that what you are about to announce to everyone? Stacey's death?"

"Yes," I said.

"Thank you for telling me first." And he left the room, just like that. I could see him walking back down the corridor to the dining room and I wondered at his strength, or was I wondering something else entirely?

I followed him back down the hall. As we entered the room everyone fell quiet as if they knew something was afoot. Before I had a chance to sit down Darcy stood up and said, "There has been an incident at the station. I have asked Cordi to explain. She has some degree of expertise in the subject." His stiff staccato sentences drummed in my ears. What was I going to say? Voluntarily or not, Darcy had just shown our hand. Since my expertise was in murder someone was going to put two and two together.

I looked around the room.

"It is with great sadness that I must inform you that Stacey has died."

I watched their faces, ranging from surprise to sadness to very little emotion, and I let their voices of concern wash over me until it was the right time to move on.

"I found her earlier this evening in her cabin while you all waited in the truck."

"What happened to her?" asked Wyatt.

"How did she die?" asked Jayne. That universal question that people instinctively want to know when they hear of a death. Is it because they can discount the death if it happened in some fashion where the deceased could be blamed? Where you then feel safe to say that couldn't happen to me?

"I found her collapsed in her chair."

"Was she ill?" Melanie asked. Everybody swung their gaze to her. "I mean, she looked ill ..." she added lamely.

"Not that I know of, except for the stomach flu," I said.

"Heart attack then, or maybe something else?" Jayne again.

"Can't tell," I said, staying as vague as I could. I looked at Jayne closely. What something else?

"Can't tell or won't tell?" said Jayne.

I glanced over at Darcy, wondering where Jayne was going with this. But all he did was an eyebrow shrug. I was on my own.

"Darcy told me you're a bit of an amateur sleuth — that you have solved a couple of murders in your time," said Jayne. I glanced at Darcy again. The eyebrow shrug was joined by a shoulder shrug.

"Your point being?"

"It seems weird that a complete stranger should be telling us about our esteemed director and that that stranger should have credentials in the homicide department. Coincidence? Given your credentials it just seems to follow that the big question here is: Was Stacey murdered?"

There was a collective intake of breath from everyone in the room, including myself. What had made her think it was murder? It couldn't just have been my reputation and Darcy's dithering, could it? And with eight faces, each showing varying degrees of concern and fear, staring up

at me, what was I going to say next? I'm sure they wondered too and could probably read it in my face. I felt like
throttling Darcy but at least I hadn't been caught out in
a lie — yet. It is usually always tricky to weasel your way
out of a lie. So I said what seemed right, "Yes. She was
suffocated." Plain and simple.

The room erupted. I watched in fascination as all my
suspects reacted to the reality of murder in their midst.
Everyone seemed surprised by the news in my quick glance
around the hall. At least, no one was tipping their hand.

Rosemary said, "If Stacey was murdered, then who
murdered her?"

The room went quiet. Sam stood up quickly and
looked around the room. "Someone in this room must
have done it."

The words had such a final feel to them, as if answering the last curtain call before everyone's life changed.
No one said a word but I'd have given a lot to know
what they were all thinking. Time for damage control.

"We can't know who did it and, as you know, there
are many others on this island who might have done it."

"But no one as easily as any of us," said Jayne. "Let's
not sugar coat this. We have a murderer in our midst on
an island that has been evacuated. We're on our own."
She turned and stared at me. "I'm still not clear on why
you're the one standing up there telling us all this."

Darcy finally came to my rescue. "You said yourself she's solved some Canadian murders. We need her
expertise."

"We need a director to handle this, not an assistant
and certainly not a newcomer."

"The director's dead, in case you hadn't noticed."

She glared at him but ignored what he had said. Instead she said, "So you took it upon yourself to carry out the duties of the director without conferring with anyone but this stranger?" And she inclined her head at me.

"There is no clear line of command," said Darcy.

"Oh, but there is and I'm it." She looked around at all the people in the room. "I am the only one here who has been the director of this station in the past."

"I understand you were fired. I'm not sure you are the right choice," said David.

"I was let go. There's a difference, you know."

"Not from what I heard." Jayne and David had locked eyes and I wished I could hear the unspoken words between them.

"I think Cordi is an excellent choice." I was surprised to hear David siding with me. I guess I thought he should have been too distraught over his sister to care about much else.

He continued. "She's a qualified outsider so she can be objective about all the infighting that goes on around here."

It was unanimous except for Jayne, who nonetheless seemed resigned to the situation. I was to deal with the police and everything to do with Stacey's death and everyone was to co-operate with me.

Now what? I thought as everyone wandered away, taking their secret thoughts with them. Even Darcy had left me standing there, wondering where to begin.

"You've got to call the police, Cordi," said Martha. I smiled. She had an uncanny ability to read my mind sometimes. She handed me her cellphone, but there was no reception, which wasn't surprising given the state of the weather and where we were.

"So who did it?" Straight as an arrow is Martha. I thought about it for a minute and realized I'd been thinking about it for a lot longer than a minute.

"Did anyone act weird when I told them it was murder?"

Martha squished up her face and said, "Melanie started to sneeze, Wyatt coughed or maybe choked, Jayne looked angry, and David looked sick. Don't know about everybody else because Jayne got up and spilled her guts."

I tried to remember, tried to recreate the scene but it was strangely elusive. "We have to secure the crime scene."

"How do we do that?"

"I don't know. I guess we find some tape or something and maybe a lock for the door?"

Martha looked out the window but the thunderous rain had blotted out the view. "Do you think we really need to? Who's going to go snooping around a crime scene in weather like this?"

"We are."

"But shouldn't we wait for Duncan?"

"I haven't been able to alert him yet, supposing he's fool enough to still be on the island." Which meant I was probably going to have to brave the weather to get him. We had to get Stacey up to the refrigerator and that meant getting Duncan to oversee the technicalities of her death.

"Don't even think about it," said Martha. "Give the weather time to calm down a bit. Let's just go find Darcy and get that padlock."

She had a point, so I didn't argue. We eventually found Darcy in the lounge with David. They were standing over by the window, hunched over in conversation. They started when we came in as if we'd caught them with their hands in the cookie jar. I called out to Darcy and he left David standing there without a word, which seemed rather rude. After I explained to him what we wanted he led us down into the bowels of the research station to a poky windowless little room that smelled of oil and sawdust. Along one wall was a workbench full of tools tossed there by the last user, and the wall was lined with more. There was a portable table saw and a drill press and a few other assorted portable power tools. It was obviously a communal room that everyone used, and no one particularly cared about because everything seemed out of place. Which is a polite way of saying it was a mess. Darcy zeroed in on a four drawer see-through plastic cabinet and began pulling out the drawers. Martha and I began rifling through a number of toolboxes stored on the floor. As I pulled out a miniature combo lock, with a little tag giving the combo — someone wasn't so disorganized — I looked over at Darcy and said, "What happened with the evacuation alert?"

He looked over his shoulder at me. "What do you mean?"

"I would have thought Stacey would have taken the alert, not you."

"She did. But she asked me to get everyone organized for a 4:00 pickup."

"What time was that?"

"3:00 in the morning, I think." He had gone back to rifling through the drawers.

"And when did you last see her alive?"

He turned around, a honking big clasp in his hand, and said, "Must have been around 9:30 at night. I was up getting a snack and she was having a tête-à-tête with her brother. They were arguing about some famous baseball player. Anyway, I didn't stick around. They seemed like they wouldn't be happy if I had interrupted them. So I went back to my cabin, and yes I was alone until the alert came in."

I smiled as he handed Martha the clasp, some serious-looking Robertson screws, a portable drill, a Robertson bit, and a roll of bright orange marking tape.

"I'd help," he said, "but I'm all thumbs when it comes to tools." And with that he left.

"Convenient excuse," said Martha uncharitably. I wondered about that. He had given me, without hesitation, exactly what I needed. I extricated the clasp from her hand and held up the little lock to see if it was big enough to go through the hasp. Just.

"That lock won't stop a no-see-um," said Martha when she caught sight of it.

"Got a better idea?"

Martha shook her head.

As we left I noticed a box of latex gloves and swiped two, as well as a pair of safety goggles. We headed back up the stairs to the dining room. Melanie was sitting at one of the tables picking away at some food. Sam was sitting at another table with his back to her. I wondered what had happened to split them apart like that.

I hauled my hood up over my head, put the tools and the clasp and lock in my voluminous pockets, and headed out the door, Martha on my tail. It didn't seem to be as windy or as rainy as before, but maybe that was just wishful thinking. We navigated down the slippery stairs, walked across the clearing, and joined the trail leading to Stacey's cabin. It didn't look as ominous in the grey light of day, just kind of derelict, with one of its wooden shutters hanging loose — until I remembered what was inside. Without even conferring we decided to do the lock and tape first. I don't think either of us wanted to go into that cabin. It didn't take too long to get it done with two people, but it was pretty wet and the rain had trickled down my wrists and in under my jacket sleeves and soaked my arms as I drilled the holes and then screwed in the screws. It was pretty clammy.

When we were done I quickly opened the door and stepped inside before I had a change of heart. It was dim but I could make her out lying there on the floor. The room leapt to life as Martha switched on the light, its harshness spilling over onto Stacey as she lay there where we had left her, the duct tape still partially stuck to her face like some grotesque growth. Martha was rummaging around in her rainsuit looking for something, which was very distracting because I was trying to go through all the things that the police would do that I might be able to do — which was basically stand and stare — take everything in. I jerked as a light flashed and took a deep breath when I realized it was just Martha taking more pictures. We'd made quite a mess of the place while trying to save someone who had been probably long past saving. I took out the gloves and put them on.

I tried to ignore Stacey and her gaping mouth and started scanning the room for anything unusual. I began with Stacey herself and, apart from the duct tape and the raw wrists, there was nothing until I saw the hand of the wrist Darcy had untied. It was clutching a necklace. As I took a closer look, pushing the fingers out of the way with a pencil, I saw that it was a MedicAlert necklace for diabetes. Had she managed to jerk it off her attacker without them noticing? I had a vague sensation that something was missing but I couldn't put my finger on it. I turned and looked at her bed, which took up almost half the room even though it was pushed up against two walls. One wall was dedicated to a statue of Christ on the cross. *So she was devout*, I thought, and wondered how she reconciled the logic of a scientific mind with the fantasy of religion. She had a desk that ran the length of the other wall and a tall-backed leather swirly chair. It was impossible to tell what was our mess and what was Stacey's.

The floor was bare, uneven, rough wood but it was covered in a cascade of pens, all cheap BIC pens, except one sleek green Parker and an old-fashioned fountain pen. An old and battered Campbell's soup tin lay beside them. Maybe she had reached out to defend herself and had knocked the can and all the pens to the floor. But then again it could have been me and Darcy struggling to get her to the floor.

I sniffed the air. Something was sticking out from under her bed and I moved closer to take a look. It was white cheesecloth folded over many times to make a wad. I got down on my hands and knees and took a sniff. Definitely the source of the sweet, cloying smell I had smelled earlier. Chloroform. While I was on the floor I looked under the bed. There were a slew of medical texts, their spines all facing me, and a stack of what looked like research papers, although I couldn't tell what they were about. I stood up and brushed some dead flies and what looked like a squished cricket from my pants, a testament to her cleaning abilities, or lack thereof.

Martha was taking photographs of Stacey and I watched as she snapped pictures of the chair where Stacey had been sitting. I looked more carefully, sure that something was missing but I couldn't put my finger on what. When Martha had finished there wasn't much left for us to do. We locked up and strung some tape across the door to make it look official. The rain had lightened a bit and I decided to go for Duncan before things got worse. The fact that Martha didn't even offer to come with me made me realize that even though the rain had slackened it was still a wildly wicked day out there. It wasn't the kind of day one would choose to venture out in. But venture I did. I had a hard time getting the bike started and had to stop and wipe the rain from my eyes several times before I remembered the safety goggles. There was a lot of puddling on the road from the rain and quite a few branches had fallen across the track. Some of them I moved but I had to bushwhack around others. Duncan had said he was off the main road — which was pretty simple because there was only one main road running north and south with driveways running off it. I already knew how to get to Hunter's so I figured it would be a breeze to find the first road past it going left. But of course it wasn't simple. There seemed to be quite a few roads or driveways and I had to stop and get off the bike to read some of the signs. I finally found it. A tiny little sign half hidden in the palmetto. "Macpherson." I drove down the untamed driveway and broke out into a clearing. At first I couldn't see the house because it was so well hidden by the trees. And when I did see it I wasn't sure what I was looking at. I walked closer, my heart beginning to race when I realized that I couldn't see the house because an enormous live oak had some crashing down upon it, splitting the roof in two. I began to run.

chapter ten

I called Duncan's name but the wind just sucked it up before it even had a chance to leave my mouth. When I got closer I could see that the tree had fallen across one end of the building from front to rear, buckling it. A set of stairs wound their way up to the house like miniature switchbacks. I looked at them carefully. They didn't seem to have tilted or swayed out of true so I cautiously began to climb them, calling Duncan's name, more out of the need to be useful than for the good it would do.

For some reason I started counting the number of steps as I climbed them, the rain clouding my goggles and the wind slashing at my face in fits and starts. At one point I heard the tree groan and shift and thought I heard someone cry out. When I finally reached the top the house looked untouched from where I stood, the front door snug in its frame, the windows unharmed. I opened the door and walked in. It smelled like hamburgers and French fries, which made me feel quite desperate, and I called out his name again. His cottage was a bungalow, long and lean, and the tree had taken out the living-room wall and whatever lay beyond it. It had also knocked over a large corner cupboard that was now partially held up by a corner of the sofa. As I moved into his living room I could see the tree, its wet, glistening bark making it look like some monstrous creature, its limbs so incongruous inside the house. I called his name again.

"Get me the god damned hell out of here." His gruff, muffled, and angry voice came from somewhere behind the sofa and to me, in that moment, it sounded like a symphony. I moved quickly, rounded the sofa and there he was, sprawled on the floor, both his legs pinned by the weight of the corner cupboard. It had fallen sideways across him and as I came around to help him he said, "You're going to have to get my car jack down in the garage. You'll never be able to lift it yourself. It's solid oak."

"Are they broken?"

"My legs? No, I don't think so. The sofa broke the fall, not my legs."

I left then. On the way back up with the jack I counted more stairs than I had the first time.

I positioned the jack at the top and middle of the cupboard and started ratcheting it up. I went slowly, afraid I was going to hurt him, but Duncan told me to speed things up, so I did. Once his legs were free he insisted upon extricating himself without my help and plopping down into his sofa with a huge sigh.

"What took you so long?" he said and smiled.

"How long?" I said.

"How long what?" but I knew he knew what I meant.

"Two hours, give or take, and don't go telling me I should have evacuated because unless my eyes are deceiving me you haven't evacuated either."

"Lucky for you." It came out sounding sarcastic but it was anything but. "You could have died here," I said. "It could have been a week before anyone found you."

"Not with friends like you, Cordi."

"But I wasn't around those other times you didn't evacuate."

"And I didn't get pinned by a tree."

"You're incorrigible, Duncan." I gave him a hug.

He started gingerly rubbing the circulation back into his legs. "Nothing broken," he said, "but they're going to be awfully sore for a while." He shifted his weight on the sofa and turned to look at me.

"Why did you come?" he asked.

"How well do you know Stacey?"

"Not well. We say hello when we meet on the beach, but that's about it. Why?"

"I found her dead in her cabin early this morning."

He sighed. "Too bad, but she really didn't look very well this visit. I suppose that's why you're here. You want me to come and tell you how she died since the police won't be coming out in this weather."

"Oh, we already know how she died, Duncan."

He raised his hairy eyebrows at me.

"She was murdered."

The eyebrows plummeted into a scowl. "Oh c'mon, Cordi. Not again."

I thought about my last murder investigation, onboard an Arctic cruise ship, and how Duncan and

Martha hadn't believed me when I cried murder. This time it was more cut and dried though.

"It's the real thing, Duncan. She was suffocated." I filled him in on all the details of the crime scene as he slowly got to his feet and tried out his legs.

"So you're saying someone comes to her cabin and knocks her out with gauze soaked presumably in chloroform. They then tie her arms to the chair and duct tape her mouth and nose shut. Jesus. Why would someone do that?"

"That's what we have to find out."

"We?"

"Well, I've been appointed the person in charge of the investigation until the police come and we need a TOD before we move her into a refrigerator."

"How on earth is she going to fit into a refrigerator?" asked Duncan.

"It's a walk-in," I said, and he grimaced. "Will you come?"

He looked around at the wreck of his cottage and sighed. "Well, I can't stay here," he said, and as if to accent his observation the tree shifted again and his once cozy little cottage shuddered in sympathy.

It took me awhile to find Duncan's medical bag — he wouldn't leave without it — and it took Duncan a long time to get down all those stairs. Getting his leg up and over my bike to straddle it left us both sweating but he did it, and we made it back to the station as the wind strengthened. I wondered how much stronger it would get and decided that that line of thinking was counterproductive.

I led Duncan straight to Stacey's cabin but it took me awhile to key in the combo since the rain kept getting in my eyes. I had left my goggles at Duncan's.

Duncan was getting impatient by the time I finally got it. "Dear Cordi, that lock wouldn't stop a feather."

This time I had a response to that observation. "It's the authority it represents that counts," I said. I left him there with his medical bag to go and get help with Stacey and find out where Duncan could sleep for the night. Outside was a howling madhouse and getting worse by the second as I braced myself against the wind and staggered to the stairs. It must have been 6:00 in the afternoon — dinnertime — but it felt more like 10:00 because it was so dark.

I struggled up the stairs and into the dining room, shutting the door on the hurricane with relief. The room was full. Everyone seemed to have congregated here rather than be alone in their cabins, or maybe they were just waiting for dinner. Darcy caught sight of me, and extricated himself from a conversation with Sam, and came to join me.

"Duncan's down with Stacey," I said. "We need help carrying her up." I scanned the room. This was not the time for women's lib — this was the time for male strength. Wyatt and Darcy were there and so were David and Trevor.

"People," Darcy's voice rang out and the rumble of conversation ceased. "The coroner's here and he's looking at Stacey right now. We need a contingent to help carry her up to the fridge. I'm in. Who else is?"

David put up his hand. I looked over at Trevor, who shrugged and said, "Bad back. Sorry." I wondered if a shrimper could shrimp with a bad back. I looked at Wyatt, who just stared at Darcy as if he was a particularly interesting species of cockroach.

Darcy stared him down and said, "Wyatt?"

Wyatt dragged a hand down his face. "In the interests of all our backs, not to mention crime-scene protocol, I think she should stay where she is until the police come."

Darcy hesitated and then regrouped. "In the interests of dignity, she needs to be brought up here."

"Has anyone called the police on this one?" retorted Wyatt.

Darcy inclined his head at me and I had one of those moments of panic when you are not sure what to say. I had forgotten to try after that first attempt.

Darcy coughed and turned back to Wyatt, after giving me a wild glance. "There's no cellphone service," he said.

"Rather convenient, isn't it?" asked Wyatt.

"I'm not sure what you are getting at."

"Maybe you murdered Stacey or Ms Cordi O'Callaghan did and destroying the crime scene will destroy any evidence against you."

Darcy stood with his jaw resting on his chest and I leapt in. "Every inch of Stacey's cabin and Stacey herself has now been systematically photographed and the pathologist is looking at Stacey right now. We will only be moving her — the rest of the crime scene will be intact."

"Don't get your knickers in such a knot," said Wyatt with a smile, which of course just made me more defensive. "Let's get on with it or we'll miss dinner," he said. I looked over at David to see his reaction to all this but he had turned his back to us and was peering out the rain-soaked window.

"Whoever helps with Stacey is excused from helping to make dinner tonight," said Darcy. I raised an eyebrow at him. It seemed a rather insensitive thing to say, given the circumstances. He misconstrued my raised eyebrow and said, "The cooks left on the last boat."

That meant we'd all have to pitch in to feed ourselves. I wondered for a moment what sort of meals these disparate people were capable of making. Food has its own fingerprints, its own life, and it could reveal a lot about a person. Meat and potatoes: conservative, doesn't like surprises; spicy food: a traveller, adventurous; raw squid and goat's blood: an extreme eater. But on second thought maybe it was less like fingerprints and more like astrology.

"Time to go get Stacey," said Darcy and headed for the door. As I stepped outside after him it was as if nature lay coiled like a snake waiting to strike, her ragtag band of wind and rain and clouds all waiting in the shadows, ready. Someone gripped my shoulder hard and said, "Stairs are for walking down." I turned and caught a glimpse of Wyatt behind me before I headed down the stairs.

I caught up to Darcy at the bottom of the stairs as he tried to skirt the large puddle that had sprouted there. "Why haven't you called the police?" he asked, trying to keep his voice flat and cold but failing miserably. He was just too friendly a guy to hold grudges.

"There really was no cell service," I said lamely. "And then I forgot."

"How can you forget something as momentous as murder, unless perhaps you wanted to." He pinned me with his accusing eyes.

"Jesus. You think I killed her?" I squawked. His face softened as he looked at me and shrugged, but he didn't retract the question and I didn't deign to answer.

Duncan was sitting on Stacey's bed, writing in a notebook, when Darcy opened the door and we both walked in, leaving the rest of our contingent standing in the doorway — there wasn't enough room for them to come in. I introduced them all to Duncan, who nodded his head in acknowledgement and said, "She was suffocated."

Wyatt snorted and loudly whispered, "We knew that already."

Duncan looked up and stared at him. Even an iron rod would have withered under that look, but Wyatt was unfazed and just snorted again.

"As I was saying," Duncan continued, "she was suffocated. Probably around 3:00 a.m., judging by her core body temperature."

He looked at me. "Looks like we have another murder, Cordi."

"Another?" asked Wyatt in a startled voice.

"He doesn't mean another one here on the island," Darcy said defensively.

"God, no," said Duncan as he eyeballed Wyatt. "Cordi here has two solved murders under her belt. I was referring to those."

Wyatt made a point of looking at my belt, but he kept quiet. I looked at them all standing there and wondered if any of them was about to help carry up the body of the woman they had murdered. It sent a jolt through me to realize we were trapped on a deserted barrier island with a murderer roaming free. Darcy cleared his throat and said, "Let's move her."

She was in full rigor. The four of us each took a leg or a shoulder, but she was stiff and unwieldy and very heavy. As I struggled with my side of her we exited the cabin and headed for the stairs. Duncan had tried to take my place but I had vetoed him — not only was he terribly unfit with a heart condition but he had just sustained a blow to his legs and his ego, both of which must have been painful. He contented himself with directing us up the stairs, which were suddenly way narrower than I remembered. We carried Stacey, frozen into position as if sitting in a chair, which of course she had once been, and made it up the stairs without a stop — not that we could have stopped even if we had wanted to. Putting her down on the stairs would have meant picking her up again.

We arrived in the dining room, hot, dishevelled, and out of breath. We sat her down in a chair and stood back to catch our breath. She sat there with her chin on her chest as if she had dozed off. She was wearing very feminine pink rose pajamas, and I wondered with sadness if she had ever worn them for someone else or were they just for herself, or for the memory of someone long gone, or someone long lost? I could see her raw, bare wrists and the MedicAlert necklace grasped in her hand. Her feet were bare. Had she been awakened to her death or had she already been awake to confront her murderer? Had she struggled? I thought back to the cabin before we mucked it up. It hadn't looked as if a struggle had taken place. That might have been because of the chloroform.

"Let's get this done, folks," said Darcy, interrupting my line of thought.

Someone had cleaned out the cooler and it was pretty straightforward moving her in there. I wondered how many times she had come to this very cooler for a pop or a sandwich and if she had ever had even an inkling that she would end up here, beside the cheese and the Diet Pepsi. It was somewhat anticlimactic afterward, when we gathered outside the cooler. We all had a drink together but everybody was guarded because the one topic we all wanted to talk about was fraught with fear and guilt. We each drifted off and I wandered down the hall to call the police in privacy. I'd put it off for long enough, and I wondered if Darcy really believed I had killed her based on the fact that I hadn't called the police.

I poked my nose into an empty lab and sat down at a desk full of papers. I picked up the phone. I was actually surprised to get a dial tone and nearly hung up, but I resisted the urge — after all, the phone call had to be made. When I said I had a murder to report I was put through to a Detective Kennedy. While I was waiting I scanned the desk I was sitting at. There was a paper poking out from inside a medical textbook. I tugged on it, glanced about guiltily, and then looked at it. It was a lab report with Sam's signature, detailing the makeup of some substance that was foreign to me. And a second sheet with a diagram of a chemical formula. The results looked benign and I lost interest as Detective Kennedy came on the line.

"Tell me everything," he said, and I could hear the soft tap-tap sound of a computer keyboard as he inputted my somewhat creatively edited story. He interrupted me a number of times to clarify some things and then said, "It's anarchy here on the mainland. I won't be able to send a team out for at least three days. We're too busy rescuing the injured to do anything about the dead."

"Three days?" I asked, thinking about Stacey in the cooler.

"You'll need to secure the crime scene. Don't touch anything, or move anything until we get there."

Okay. So I forgot to tell him everything, I thought, wondering what to say now. I thought about Stacey and blurted out — "What about Stacey?"

"Who's Stacey?"

"The murder victim," I said impatiently.

"The alleged murder victim," he said, and I made a face at the phone. "Don't touch her."

"But it's forty degrees Celcius outside," I pleaded.

Before I could say anything more he begged off saying he had an important call coming through and he had to take it.

I hung up and stared at my cell, thinking about Stacey and the cooler. And what the cops would say when they heard the truth.

chapter eleven

I was lost in thought and not trying very hard to get found when I heard someone clear their throat. I looked up to see Wyatt leaning up against the door jamb. I wondered how long he had been there. Instinctively I picked up the lab report and then realized I couldn't exactly put it back where I found it with him standing there staring at me.

"Do you always snoop around other people's desks?" He smiled at me, slow, easy, and nasty.

"Do you always sneak up on people unannounced?" I retorted.

"Always," he said, the smile now reaching his eyes.

"And is that what you were doing when you sneaked up on Stacey and murdered her?" I surprised myself by saying that. I had no evidence to justify the question, especially framed in that way.

I could see the muscles of his cheek start to vibrate as he clenched his jaw. "I was nowhere near her when she died," he said, his voice low and even. He stared at me.

"You have your fucking nerve to accuse me of murder," he added, his anger barely under control.

"Where were you when she died?"

He suddenly laughed. "Depends on *when* she died."

"About three in the morning."

I could see the contempt in his eyes as he decided whether to answer me or not.

"Three in the morning." He laughed again. "Where the hell do you think I was at that hour?"

He was digging in his heels for some reason so I took another tack. "Who hired you to come and do the vaccinations?"

He was taken off guard by my change of topic and bit his lip, either in exasperation or annoyance. "The Island Association. They were given a mandate to get the horses vaccinated so they wouldn't get pregnant. I complied." He raised his hands and shrugged at the same time, the anger gone like a water drop in fire.

"I understand there were a lot of islanders against the vaccinations."

"So?"

"So maybe Stacey was against the vaccinations and you didn't like that."

He looked at me and laughed. "What sort of god-forsaken motive is that?" He laughed again, pushed off from the doorframe, and held out his hand at me. I frowned. "Could you hand me the medical text, please?"

I glanced down at it. It was a book on neurodegenerative diseases and Stacey had stuck her address label on it. I took a deep breath. So this was Stacey's desk and here was Wyatt wanting something from it before I had had a chance to search it, or at least before the police had.

"I'm no expert but I think it had better just stay where it is until the police come."

He slowly dropped his hand and then raised it in a salute. "Your wish is my command," he said, but something stirred behind his eyes like a monster shifting in its sleep, and I watched with some misgiving as he vanished into the hallway, half expecting him to come back and harangue me some more.

I reached for the medical text, wondering why he was so interested. Or perhaps it was because of what was in it — the lab report with the chemical formula. It occurred to me that maybe Stacey had hidden it for some reason. I pulled out the sheet again and looked at it, but my organic chemistry wasn't up to it. I looked at Stacey's computer and realized I couldn't even search the Internet for the formula because it was a diagram. On impulse I folded and pocketed it. I glanced outside. The wind had died down and the rain had stopped. It was dinnertime, but I didn't feel like eating after seeing Stacey dumped in the cooler so I closed her door and then couldn't figure out how to seal the room from intruders.

"Just about everyone has access to all these doors." Darcy was walking down the corridor toward me and doing a good job of reading my mind again.

As he approached he pulled out a hasp lock like the one we had used on Stacey's cabin, and began screwing it into place.

"It seems ridiculous to do this," he said, "but I guess with Stacey's killer still out there it's for the best." He put the screwdriver back in his pocket and fished out another pint-sized lock with two keys. He handed one key to me, hesitated a moment, and then handed the other one to me as well.

"Best you keep them both," he said. "I don't want anyone accusing me of tampering with the evidence and you are pretty much in the clear for this murder."

"That's not what you said earlier," I pointed out.

He sighed. "Sorry about that. I was kind of traumatized. In hindsight it's pretty hard to believe that you would kill a complete stranger and have no motive, unless of course you are a contract killer?"

I laughed. But I had the strange feeling that he was half in jest and all in earnest.

I changed the subject. "Can you walk me through the evacuation protocol?"

"I don't understand," he said.

"Who gets the call to evacuate?"

"We've already been through this."

"Humour me."

"Stacey gets the call and then she alerts me and I'm supposed to organize everybody."

"So what happened the other night? How did she sound?"

I saw a look of puzzlement and then something else flit across his face before he said, "She texted me."

"She texted you? Something as important as that and she texted you? Why didn't you say that earlier?"

"Yeah, it does seem odd now that you mention it, but she knows I carry my cellphone everywhere I go and that I wouldn't miss a call. My beeper sounds like a turbo jet at that hour of the morning. She just told me to take care of the evacuation, that she was going to stay and take care of the station."

"Why did you ask me to go and get her then?"

"I was hoping she'd change her mind."

He shrugged and started to turn away.

"What was the last text message from her besides the evacuation alert?"

"Why would you want to know that?"

"Because maybe we can pinpoint the time of death better."

"She didn't text me but she did call me around 11:30." He laughed.

"She said she had spilled her box of crickets all over the floor and they were driving her crazy. She wanted to know if I had any useful ideas of how to get them all."

"And did you?"

"No. I just told her she'd have to stomp on them. I couldn't stop laughing though. Those crickets are as loud as hell."

"What was she doing with a whole bunch of crickets?"

"They were Roger's food," he said unhelpfully. When I looked puzzled he said, "Her snake."

"I never saw a snake in her cabin," I said.

"I let Mel take it."

I wondered what else he'd let people take before I'd secured the scene, but I dropped it and said, "Do you know if she had any enemies, anyone who would want to kill her?"

He looked at me strangely, and I thought maybe he hadn't heard, but he sighed and said, "She had people who didn't like her, but no one who would have wanted to kill her. I mean, that is kind of drastic, isn't it?" He pinned me with his moss green eyes and then looked away. "I've got to go."

I touched his arm and he turned back to me, struggling to control his impatience.

I pulled out the little diagram and carefully unfolded it. "Do you have any idea what this means?" I handed it to him and was surprised by the furtive look on his face as he took it from me.

"Where did you get this?" he asked.

Before I could answer Sam came out of the next office and swept us down the hall to dinner, but not before I snatched the paper back from Darcy just as it was about to disappear into his pocket. He glanced at me, flustered, but he let me take the paper. I thought we were done then, but he hung back and said, "I don't think you need to try and solve this crime, Cordi. All I meant was for you to liaise with the police and oversee the sealing of the crime scene." And he smiled then, a smile so fast and fleeting that I barely saw it before he walked down the hall, his hands clenched at his sides.

I still didn't feel like dinner so I bailed out and headed back to my cabin, where I lay down and thought about Stacey until I fell asleep.

A humungous snort from Martha woke me up at about 5:00 in the morning and I couldn't get back to sleep, even though I wanted to. The sky was just beginning to lighten and the wind was now just a dull moan through the trees. It seemed that the hurricane had veered and missed us almost completely, but the mainland had not been so lucky. I looked over at Martha, who was sleeping with wild abandon, her arms flung out above her head and her dark curly hair sprawled all over the pillow. I wondered how I had managed to sleep through her coming home last night. It occurred to me that if I could sleep through that then probably anyone with a roommate could conceivably sleep through it too. Doubly so if they were heavy sleepers.

It took me all of two minutes to get dressed and snag a long-sleeved jacket — more for the bugs than the temperature — and exit the cabin, holding the screen door as I shut it so it wouldn't bang. I was headed toward the stairs to the mess when movement caught my eye. Someone was sneaking between two cabins, slowly, as though they didn't want to be caught. I stopped and squinted through the brush but I couldn't make out who it was and they had stopped moving, like a deer on the alert. I almost turned away, but something prompted me to move in the direction of whoever it was and say *good morning* in a loud whisper. The figure remained still for some five seconds and then slowly walked out of the shadows toward me. It was Rosemary. The dawn caught her red hair, burnishing it like fire and lighting up the lemon yellow of the jacket she had draped around her neck.

She nodded at me. "Hello, Cordi," she said in a voice that made it sound as though she wished she were anywhere but with me. She was wearing a pair of enormous sunglasses but even they could not hide the new purple welt under her left eye. Involuntarily I gasped and she seemed to shrink to an even smaller size than she already was.

"Who did this to you?" I asked.

"No one," she said defiantly.

"Another cabin door?" It was mean, but I felt I had to say it. When she didn't answer I said, "You don't have to go through this alone, you know. There are people who can help you."

She looked at me then with a faraway gaze that made me realize I didn't know what the hell I was talking about. She was trapped by something that I could only fathom.

I tried another tack. "How long has this been going on?"

She shook her head. "I don't know what you are talking about." But I could tell by her eyes that she knew exactly what I was saying.

"You don't have to live like this."

"Live like what? I'm just a klutz, that's all."

"A klutz who gets beaten on a regular basis."

She suppressed a sob and looked at me with some desperation. Time ticked by and I thought I heard a Painted Bunting somewhere in the distance and realized I should be in the field.

"I don't know what to do," she abruptly said as she reached her hand up under her glasses and wiped her eye. "Wyatt doesn't mean to ..." She put her hand over her mouth as if she had said too much.

I wondered what sort of man could do this to such a vulnerable young woman, what kind of man would think it all right to beat the hell out of her.

"You have choices," I said, wondering if I should hug her or something.

"You don't understand," she cried out in a wailing moan. "I have no choices."

"You always have choices," I said.

"Not when I love him." She turned and started running toward her cabin, her lemon yellow jacket flapping in the breeze, making her look like the sad and sorry apparition that she was.

I sat down on the bottom steps up to the mess and gazed across at the live oaks, their leaves shattering the newborn sunlight into a hundred thousand shards. It was odd not to hear the roaring of the wind, and I wondered what the seas were like and when the police would come.

"Penny for your thoughts?"

I looked up to find David standing over me.

"You're up early," I said.

"I could say the same for you."

I went for the jugular. "Was your sister ill?"

I saw him clench his jaw as he opened his hands in an all-encompassing gesture, saying, "Not that I know of — I mean other than the flu."

"It's just that I saw some medical textbooks under her bed — not the sort of thing a botanist would keep, don't you think?"

"She had a lot of interests. What can I say?"

"That she was a whole hell of a lot sicker than anyone knew. You were her brother. You of all people would know." I wondered why I was pushing so hard, why it was important but all I could see was that pasty white complexion and the dull eyes of someone very ill. My grandmother had looked like that in the months before she died.

David gave a little snort and smoothed back his white circlet of hair. "I don't really see what Stacey's health, ill or otherwise, has to do with her death. She was suffocated."

I must say I actually shared David's sentiments, but if I have learned anything in the investigation of a murder it's that anything goes and any question could lead to the solving of the crime. So I up and said, "Was she depressed?"

David looked at me with a puzzled look that melted into patient resignation. "No more than usual. She's carried her depression around with her half her life, almost like a trophy sometimes."

I bristled at that — anyone who has ever suffered from depression would never call it a trophy, an albatross maybe but never a trophy. I was beginning to see why brother and sister did not see eye to eye.

"Where are you going with this anyway?" he asked.

"Just trying to get as many facts as I can and hope that some of them turn out to be relevant."

"I don't know why you're even bothering. The police will be here in a few days. Leave it to them."

He turned to go but I said, "Where were you when your sister was murdered?"

"You've got to be kidding. You think I killed my sister?"

"I'm just trying to rule you out."

"Well, good luck doing that with me or anyone else for that matter. We were all in bed asleep."

"Do you have a roommate?"

"No, as a matter of fact I don't."

"Too bad," I said. "They might have given you an alibi. What were you talking about to Stacey when you first arrived on the island?"

"Regular nosey-parker aren't you?" he said.

"She seemed shocked by whatever you were telling her."

"And whatever I was telling her will remain between her and me." He turned then to go up the stairs and I let him go.

I suddenly didn't feel like going up to the mess so I headed back to the cabin.

"Lord love a duck, Cordi, what are you doing up already? Even the birds aren't chirping yet." A robin gurgled somewhere right outside our cabin and she shrugged.

I sat down on my bed — there was nowhere else to sit — and looked out the window, wondering why I felt so flat. Martha turned on the light and sat down on her bed facing me. She was just about to say something when a voice came out of nowhere, catapulting my heart against my chest like a battering ram. I really was keyed up and could only guess that I was still in some kind of shock after seeing Stacey.

"Cordi, Martha, it's me." The voice was whispery.

Who the hell was me? I wondered, as the whisperer answered my question. "Duncan." What the hell was he doing up so early? Everyone seemed to be awake and I just wanted to go back to sleep.

Martha got up and let him in. "Couldn't sleep," he said. He did not look much better than I felt, and his gargantuan nose was peeling from sunburn. It looked like a potato shedding its skin. I looked at the two of them sitting side by side so comfortably and wondered if they would ever marry, or maybe it worked precisely because it was a long-distance relationship with Martha in Ottawa and Duncan an hour's drive away. I thought about the man I thought had loved me, whose job took him away to England. It seemed unbearably sad that we had been unable to make it work, when there had been so much promise.

"Paging Cordi. Come in, Cordi." Duncan's voice brought me back and I marvelled at how easily the mind can take you down dark, treacherous roads, unmarked and best untravelled. Dangerous place, the mind.

"Okay, Cordi," said Duncan, "unlike our other cases this one was definitely not made to look like an accident. Hands and feet tied, mouth and nose plastered in duct tape."

"What about her wrists? They were chafed," I said.

"Only what you would expect from someone struggling for her life." He paused and then said, "She was a sentimental woman."

"How so?"

"She wore a locket around her neck."

I remembered the locket.

"Guess what was in it?"

"A picture of Leonard Cohen?" said Martha.

Duncan grimaced. "A lock of hair," he said.

I wondered about that.

"Probably her own," said Martha.

"Why would you say that? She doesn't strike me as being a woman who would wear her own hair around her neck," I said.

Duncan chuckled.

"Okay, okay, except when it's attached to her head."

"Well, whoever's hair it is, it's baby hair," observed Duncan.

"How do you know that?"

"I can't know for sure, but it's thin and very soft, not like adult hair at all."

At that we lapsed into silence until Martha blurted out, "Okay, so Duncan says she died at 3:00 in the morning when everyone was asleep. Why didn't anyone know sooner than 4:00 when Cordi stumbled on her?"

Duncan and I blinked at Martha and waited politely for her to explain herself.

"She's the head of the station. The evacuation alert would have gone through her first. That was the time she died — around 3:00 because we evacuated at 4:00. Presumably when they couldn't raise her they would have phoned someone else, my bet's Darcy, who surely would have gone to see why she hadn't responded to an emergency phone call."

"She texted him."

"She texted him?"

"Darcy was surprised at that too but he just did what he was told."

"You know what that means don't you?" said Duncan.

"That we can't know for sure that the message came from Stacey."

"You mean the murderer could have sent it? Why would they do that?"

"To buy time," I said. "If the evacuation had gone as planned and Stacey had stayed behind it would have been days before she was found. Darcy says she texted him that she was not evacuating and to go without her."

Martha slapped her knee in frustration. "And hardly anybody is going to have an alibi for this murder. It was the middle of the night and everyone was asleep."

She had a point. We probably wouldn't be able to eliminate anybody, but I'd still have to ask just in case.

"So why would anyone want to kill her?" asked Duncan. "I mean, what do we know about her?"

"Pretty much nothing at this point. It's all questions," said Martha.

"She didn't seem like someone who would have people wanting to kill her. Actually, she just seemed sick," I said.

"She was sick," said Martha. "Darcy told me she'd been sick for the last five days with some kind of stomach flu and that she only surfaced when we arrived."

I knew that already but I remembered the medical texts under her bed and wondered if she'd been consulting them over her flu bug. Had she been a hypochondriac? And was that even pertinent?

"So that's why she hadn't met Wyatt, even though he'd been on the island for two days?"

"Yeah, that did seem strange, the manner of their meeting." She made it sound so ominous that I started laughing.

"How can you laugh, Cordi? You are probably the last one to have seen her alive."

I stopped laughing as I realized, with an acrobatic leap of my stomach, that she was likely right.

"Besides the killer," I corrected her while trying to marshal my thoughts.

"Jesus, Cordi, you don't think that I think you killed her?" said Martha in consternation.

I shook my head. "No. But others might. You have to admit it doesn't look good. I arrive back with Stacey at about 11:15, at 11:30 she calls Darcy about the crickets, and by 3:00 she is dead, having just texted Darcy — or her killer having done so."

"That's still a lot of hours unaccounted for," said Martha.

Duncan shuffled his feet and stood up. "Looks like the two of you have your work cut out for you."

He was almost out the door when I remembered the chemical formula. I hauled it out of my pocket, smoothed it out, and handed it to Duncan. "What is it?" I asked as he peered at it closely.

He took his own sweet time before answering. "Sugar," he said. "Simple unadulterated sugar."

chapter twelve

Martha actually crawled back into bed — 6:00 on the clock — but I was too wide awake so opted for an early morning stroll along the bike trails with my recording equipment. The forest was sopping wet from the torrential downpour and there were large puddles and newly minted miniature lakes across the trail and in the woods. But the air had been washed clean and was lazing around drying itself off as I skirted the water. The birds had already started to sing and I was recording a bunting when I heard the distant putt of an ATV. Having witnessed Trevor's wild careen around a blind corner I moved to one side of the path and kept walking as the vehicle moved alongside me. I glanced over and saw Jayne yelling over the noise of her machine. I recoiled, thinking she was going to say something nasty to me.

"Want a lift?" It seemed like such an anticlimactic thing to say. But she looked so friendly. She was wearing her curly hair tied back in a bouncy ponytail and looked like she'd be at home on a movie set where she was the star.

"Where are you headed?"

"I'm heading out with my turtles to do some experiments. Want to come?"

I figured I could do two birds with one stone, my research on buntings and my research on Jayne, so I said yes. I loaded my stuff into the back of her trailer. I did wonder why she was being friendly after making it known that she did not want me taking care of Stacey, but she seemed genuine enough.

"Can you do your experiments in this kind of weather?" I said.

"It's just the sea that's a mess now and the hatchlings come up no matter the weather — it just has to be warm enough to get them moving. There was a nest that came up last night and they have to be released as soon as I have finished with them, sea or no sea."

I shrugged, said "Sure," and clambered on her bike, carefully avoiding the little cooler strapped to the back.

"Bit early for a walk, isn't it? Or were you doing research?"

"Trying to find buntings," I said.

"I hope you have better luck than your hit-and-miss shenanigans with murder."

I chose to ignore the dig and said instead, "How well did you know Stacey?"

"I knew her history, of course. That she studied at both Dalhousie and McGill," she said. I looked at her then, curious at the undertone in her voice, one that was at the same time matter-of-fact but highly strained, as if both universities were subpar, or maybe she was signalling that Stacey was subpar, or maybe I was reading altogether too much into it.

"As a botanist?" I said.

"Yeah. She was Canadian. I guess that's why she went to McGill, but she never seemed like one cut out for academe. She was a loner and very hard to get to know. Rumour has it that something happened to her in her teens that soured her outlook on life."

I hate it when people drop a bomb like that and then don't follow up. They seem to derive great pleasure in forcing you to ask the big question.

"What happened to her?"

For a moment Jayne looked as though she was going to say something, but she changed her mind and merely shrugged her shoulders so I said, "Did you have a hand in hiring your replacement?"

Jayne shot me a startled look that was quickly hidden by derision. "Stacey'd been coming here for two years — my last two years as director — and the islanders made an executive decision to get rid of me and replace me with her."

"But I understand you'd burned out."

Jayne bit her upper lip and let out a long drawn-out sigh. "If that's what you want to call it," she said almost bitterly, as she swerved us down a small lane. We were barrelling down the path toward the south end of the island, careening through puddles and small lakes so that by the time we got to where Jayne was going I was sopped. The sun was still brand new on the horizon as I followed her down a trail toward the sea. She was carrying a little cooler carefully under one arm and was squirting something smelly on herself with the other. She turned and offered me some.

"The punkies hate it," she said.

I hesitated and then took some, remembering how ferocious the punkies were. The stuff smelled like a perfume factory.

When we broke out onto the beach the sea was a roiling mass of spume and splash and spindrift and spray, but the area of the beach where Jayne led me was sheltered from the wind. I watched as she walked over to a giant circle of canvas that had a grid marked on it in Magic Marker, partially hidden by sand. She had her broom with her and carefully swept the sand, deposited by the hurricane, off the canvas. Then I watched as she took a squirming hatchling from the cooler, its elongated front flippers flailing wildly and its smaller rounded rear flippers oaring the air like little rudders. I suppressed the urge to laugh as she gently placed a tiny goggle over one of its eyes, then walked out and placed it in the centre of the grid. She came back and recorded on matching grid paper the exact trail the little hatchling took as it moved off the canvas.

"This little guy has just one goggle so he can't see out of one eye. See how he is circling, trying to compensate. Turtles without goggles head straight for the sea."

It was obvious by the intensity of her concentration and the care with which she treated her study subjects just how much the research life meant to her. I looked out to sea and she followed my gaze.

"One good thing about a hurricane: it keeps the shrimp boats from going out," she said.

"Why are you so against them?" I asked.

"Because they kill my turtles. Collateral damage. They get scooped up in the nets and drown because they can't get to the surface to breathe."

"But I thought they had some kind of device to prevent that from happening."

"Turtle excluder devices, also know as TEDS. Yeah, the shrimpers hate them. They say it decreases their catch and lots of them don't use them. If they get caught they pay the fine."

"How would they ever get caught?"

"Luck or an honest observer."

"Observer?"

"Yeah. They put people on the boats to observe. To make sure any turtles that are caught are given time to get their breath before being put overboard. The shrimpers hate them too. Stacey could have told you a story or two." She let another little hatchling go and I watched it struggling to get its bearings.

"Stacey?"

"Yeah. She was just put in charge of the observers in this area last year."

"What sort of stories?"

"Oh, the usual. Bullying tactics, cold shoulders, even sexual harassment. I mean, most shrimpers are good guys, but not all of them."

"Like Trevor?"

Jayne laughed, but it was a hollow laugh. Without looking at me she took another hatchling and placed it in the centre of the grid. I waited for her to come back to me and I thought she had forgotten what we were talking about but suddenly she said, "Trevor's like all of them. Out to get a buck even if it means overfishing or causing collateral damage." She practically spit out the last two words in disdain.

"Did he and Stacey get on?"

"Are you kidding? They hated each other. Despised is more like it.

"Enough to murder Stacey?"

She slowly turned and looked at me.

"Lesser motives have killed better women than Stacey."

Jayne offered me her ATV to go to the north end and see the lighthouse. I took her up on it, and when I said I'd come back and pick her up she said not to bother, she'd stash her stuff in the hatchery and walk back by the beach, which she assured me was a much shorter route than our jouncy journey through the forest. Every ATV has its own special quirks and it took me awhile to realize I had to jiggle the key and coddle the throttle to get the thing going. It roared to life, shattering the quiet stillness of the morning. It was still early — only 7:00 as I puttered down the leaf-covered trail toward the light-house. Once I thought I heard another ATV, but above the noise of my own it could have been my imagination or my own ride playing games on me. *Too bad ATVs were so noisy*, I thought as I drove under the canopy of live oaks and all the birds that must have been there but I couldn't hear. I got lost among the warren of roads snak-ing in and around the lighthouse, but finally spied the sign of a miniature lighthouse with an arrow pointing down yet another identical-looking road. I parked the ATV in a little lay by and heard a bunting so I scrambled around for my equipment and my recorder. I spent the next half hour taping the little guy as he flew in and out of the live oaks right behind the lighthouse.

When I was done I followed a well-trodden path to a clearing and there it was, soaring above the beach and the rolling dunes like the grand old sentinel it was. But it was a sentinel that had seen better days. Its white paint was blistering as the morning sun reflected off it, showcasing all its blemishes. The red stripe that wound itself around the top had faded into a pinkish brown and the catwalk looked like something once sturdy but that you now wouldn't want to touch, let alone walk on. Part of the lighthouse was covered in a robust-looking vine that twined its way from the bottom to the very top of the structure. I wondered when the lighthouse had been retired and what they do with old and potentially dangerous lighthouses nobody wants anymore.

Just as I was heading for the door I thought I heard an ATV somewhere in the distance, but when I scanned the horizon with my ears I came up empty. The door was a huge solid wood affair, three inches thick, with an opened padlock on it that looked older than the lighthouse. I pushed open the heavy door and peered inside. There was some light streaking in from an out-of-sight second-floor window and I could see the telltale concrete spiral staircase curling up out of sight. There was a huge barrel just inside that seemed to be full of wood and other garbage. I pushed the door open further for the benefit of the light and then started up the staircase. I expected to find it swimming in dust and other debris, but evidently many islanders came here and someone obviously had taken a broom to the stairs quite recently because I could see the strokes. I climbed up to the first window and peered out through the three-foot recessed window ledge.

The brilliant white sands of Spaniel Island were so bright in the summer sun that they hurt my eyes. Dunes covered in waving sea grass swept north, where they petered out at high-tide mark. The beach was shallow and the waves had plenty of time to gather speed and energy as they roared down on the sand.

I continued climbing up and was about to place my hand on the sun-filled second window when I found myself looking into the eyes of a rattlesnake, its pupils vertical slits. It was coiled in the sun and staring at me. I wasn't sure what the striking distance of a rattlesnake was but I was taking no chances. I backed down the stairs, crossed over to the far side, and gingerly made my way up. I tried to picture the snake manoeuvring up the stairs and couldn't do it. I wondered if it had become lost and then something had frightened it, inspiring it to climb all those stairs. But then, it seemed perfectly content basking in the sun. I reached the second floor, which once must have been the keeper's living and dining areas — now totally devoid of human life except for me. When I finally reached the top there was a gaping hole where the lamp used to be, but the sun shone in on the bank of windows that encircled the space. It was quite a view of sun and sand and sea and surf and sea grass — so exotic and ageless.

And then I really did hear an ATV coming my way. Had I been in the big city all alone in a deserted lighthouse I would have been on my guard, but this was Spaniel Island; what could happen here? Then I remembered Stacey…. The ATV grew silent and so did I. There was a long scraping noise, followed by the bang of a closing door. The lighthouse door.

I went to the window and looked out. I couldn't see anyone but I yelled out to let them know I was in the lighthouse. No one stepped back to look up at me. I heard an ATV cough to life. Why would anyone come to the lighthouse for the sole purpose of closing the door? I stood and scanned the area and saw nothing. Curious, I headed back down the stairs, thinking I smelled smoke. And then my heart went in my throat as I thought about the rusty lock and whether it worked or not. But I figured I was getting ahead of myself, as I always seem to do, so I ignored all my inner negative voices and continued down the stairs. The smell of smoke was getting stronger, and by the time I reached the door it was getting hard to breathe. The barrel was on fire, exuding a thick, black, choking smoke. I skirted the fire and went for the door, wary all the time of the rattlesnake. I grabbed the handle and pulled. Nothing. I tried using both hands. Nothing. I checked the state of the hinges. Desperately I looked around for something to fight the fire with — a fire extinguisher would have been good — but there was nothing. I was trapped.

I went back up to the top of the lighthouse to look for would-be rescuers but there was no one. I was on my own. And that's when I remembered the vine. How hard would that be? I peered out the bank of windows at the catwalk and decided that thinking about it was not going to do me any good. So I wrestled the little door to the catwalk open and gingerly stepped out. Pieces of the floor were missing and I could look right down to the ground, one hundred feet away. It was a dizzying distance but I blocked it out and kept walking, testing my footing at each step, to the place where the vine was. When I reached it it looked kind of puny, but I could see fire shooting out from the door off to my left. The vine had travelled up the lighthouse and wended its way around and out of sight. I took the vine in my hand and tested it. It was thick, about the size of a tennis racquet handle, and it seemed pretty solid. I knew if I thought anymore about it I would lose my nerve. I grabbed the vine in both hands and lowered myself off the ledge. I inched my way over and down, never once looking where I was going. I got into a rhythm, a Zen-like state where the only things that existed were me, the vine, and the lighthouse. And my aching arms. And then it happened. The vine let go; in slow motion it peeled itself and me from the side of the lighthouse and gently descended to earth so that I landed with the same force as a parachutist, rolling to blunt the fall. I lay there on the ground for a while, wondering who had locked me in and why. A loud yell made me look up to see Darcy and Sam on top of what looked like an improvised fire truck — a pickup with a giant water container. Trevor was at the wheel and I watched him manoeuvre the truck close to the lighthouse. I didn't feel much like helping and they didn't know I had almost been killed. I figured I'd keep it that way.

It took them awhile to put out the fire but they managed it, in part because there wasn't any wood inside except for what was in the barrel and the door. It seemed a shame that the door had been destroyed. For all I knew it was the original.

They asked me what had happened but I said I didn't know. They didn't press and I left to find my ATV and go back to the relative safety of the research station. I was unnerved by what had just happened to me — could it have been an accident? Not a chance.

chapter thirteen

Jayne's ATV was sitting where I left it, minus a whole lot of air from one of the tires. As I got closer I could tell it had been slashed and I felt this creepy little chill go down my spine. What the hell was going on? It could be a case of mistaken identity. Whoever was after me might have thought I was Jayne. But why would anyone be after Jayne? I kicked the tire hard — it felt good to do something so useless — and then I headed back up in search of help. Sam and Darcy were gone but Trevor's truck was still in front of the lighthouse. I could see him leaning against it, having a death-defying smoke.

"All out?" I asked.

"Yeah. But if it had been my call I would have let it burn."

"But it's a historic building," I said.

"Exactly. People latch onto anything historical, throwing money and time at these albatrosses. They're sieves for money that should go elsewhere. Look at the thing. It's falling apart. It should be left to die a dignified death. Now it's just a death trap."

I looked at him quickly — could he have locked me in? — but he was idly contemplating his smelly cigarette.

"I need a ride back to the research station, if you can give me one."

"Where's your ride?"

"Flat tire."

"Let's have a look."

He reached into the truck and pulled out a small bag. I led him back to Jayne's ATV.

He let out a long, low whistle. "Jesus. Who did that?" he asked. He went up and kicked the tire. "Can't fix this. You'll need a whole new tire." He stood back and looked at the tire as if that would fix it, then said, "Hey, this is Jayne's vehicle."

"She lent it to me this morning." I watched him closely as he rubbed his forehead with the palm of his hand.

"Why would anyone want to do that to her ATV?"

"Does Jayne have any enemies?"

"Yeah. Me. But I wasn't anywhere near here." At least he was honest.

It dawned on him that I might misconstrue his remarks, and he added hurriedly, "I'd never do something like that, not in a million years."

What about two million, I thought uncharitably. Out loud I asked, "Why do you say you are Jayne's enemy?"

"She's a fucking enviro nut job. All living things are more important to her than humans. She'll save the life of a single turtle even if it means sending a child to bed hungry."

"And is that what she did?"

"What?"

"Send a child to bed hungry."

"Damn right she did and the child was mine!" He flicked his cigarette on the ground and stomped on it.

"I'm a shrimper, or I was until Jayne and Stacey came along moaning about the poor little sea turtles. They're the kind of bleeding hearts who were responsible for the TEDs and now the observers. It's harder and harder to make a living and the rules just get more and more ridiculous. I was hoping my kids would take over the boat when I retire, but there's nothing there for them."

What do you say to a man whose livelihood is threatened by conservation? Go find another job? Take it on the chin for the rest of humanity? There are no easy answers, just easy scapegoats.

"Stacey and Jayne worked on sea turtles together?"

"It was the only thing they ever agreed on, as far as I know. Both gaga over the creatures. I tell you it is not healthy when grown women take the side of a marine animal over the livelihoods of shrimpers. It's criminal."

"How do you save them then?" I asked and immediately regretted it.

"You don't," he said. I thought about all the good arguments to save creatures like sea turtles, the diversity of life, the potential cures for diseases, the esthetics, but I knew he wouldn't listen to me.

"What was their involvement?"

"Well, Jayne does research and both of them did letter-writing campaigns and things like that. Stacey went to bat for the observer program without ever asking shrimpers what it might be like to have landlubbers on their boats."

"I understand Stacey is head of that program now?"

"She made our lives miserable, always pushing for more and more observers. That and her fucking brother, always trying to win me over to the cause. Spies, that's all those observers are, and it makes us feel like scum to be treated like suspects. And Stacey was the worst, the most vocal, the most emotional, and the most vindictive in her dealings with us. Jayne was an angel compared to Stacey."

"Sounds like she made a lot of enemies."

"You'd better believe it."

"Is a sea turtle worth dying for?"

"Stacey seemed to think it was."

"And you?"

He smiled then and said, "If you are insinuating that I killed Stacey over a sea turtle then you are delusional."

"And if you killed Stacey so your children would not go to bed hungry?"

He stared at me hard and then turned and walked away.

So much for my ride.

I decided to walk back along the beach and skirted the lighthouse to get there. It still looked the same but I caught the whiff of the dank, acrid smoke that had chased me up to the catwalk. I wondered if Trevor could hate Jayne enough to do such a thing.

Judging by the sun and the heat it was around noon. I walked through a series of undulating dunes, some the size of a small car and others the size of a tractor. This was the north end of the island where the wind wandered through the dunes with reckless abandon, shaping them, shifting them, and sometimes obliterating them. There was no time for a little grass seedling to take hold, so they were naked and highly vulnerable to erosion. This particular barrier island was being eaten by the wind at the north end and built up by the wind at the south end. An island in a constant state of flux — sort of like me.

I broke out of the dunes and the beach lay before me, a white band of sand. Below the high-tide mark was a black band of compact sand, as hard as a road and as wide as a four-lane highway on a bit of a tilt. The waves were pounding in and I wondered when it would ever let up. All that power crashing on the beach and dissipating. I wondered how many people had ever thought to harness the surf.

I hiked along the wave line for a while but there wasn't much being kicked up. A few shells, a dead horse-shoe crab, and a dead seagull were about it. I headed back up above the high-tide mark thinking there would be better pickings, when I heard a putt putt and turned to look behind me. The sun was in my eyes and it wasn't until the Land Rover had come up alongside me that I realized it was Sam. I eyeballed the Land Rover — a series II — and realized it must be one of a very few trucks on the island. Most of the vehicles were ATVs.

Sam killed the motor but the sound of the surf had him yelling at me to be heard. "Trevor told me you needed a lift," he said. I was surprised. I hadn't expected that of Trevor. And where had Sam got himself another ride?

I accepted the ride because it was a chance to talk to Sam. He flapped his hand in the direction of the passenger seat and I clambered in as he moved some of his batting equipment out of the way.

We drove along the hard-packed sand, leaving barely a trace of our passage. Sam pointed at something up ahead. The tide was going out and the waves had withdrawn, leaving behind a dark object that rolled and tumbled with each passing wave. Sam drove up and circled it — a dead sea turtle. The shell was massive and was carved up by something sharp, the marks cutting across the shell seemingly at random. The enormous head was badly disfigured.

I looked up at Sam. He was shaking his head. When he saw me looking at him he said, "We are the single biggest predator of sea turtles."

I waited for more but he bent down and freed one of the creature's flippers from some seaweed. His hand gently touched a bright yellow tag attached to the flipper. "One of ours," he said and he got a pad of paper to write the number down. "God damn it." He angrily stuffed the paper into his pocket and looked at me. "This is what happens when a loggerhead sea turtle meets the propeller blades of a boat. No competition. The turtle loses every time. They can't win, what with the shrimping nets and the propeller blades, the odds are against them big time."

Stacey, Jayne, now Sam on the one side. Trevor on the other. A lot of hot blood. Had any of it spilled over into Stacey's death?

Sam didn't say much as we drove down the beach, then headed up into the dunes and then down into the interior of the island. After the roar of the wind and the waves it was deathly quiet in the woods.

"I just have to check one of my roosts," he said and swung the truck down a tiny trail that opened into a clearing. Sam pointed to an old wooden two-storey house. "The Amoses own this cottage and my bats roost in their attic. They want to exterminate them so I don't have much longer to work with them." He pointed off to my left. "That's Stacey's cottage."

I turned to look through the woods at what looked like a tiny wooden cottage painted slate blue.

"Don't know why she bought it," he said as he got out of the Land Rover and pulled a backpack out of the back. "Except for the last five days she hardly ever used it. She was married to her job. Hated being away from it all. But then sometimes she'd drop everything and come to the cottage. Sort of like an escape, I guess, but a very expensive one."

I looked up at the cottage, which was ninety percent window, and as I did someone came out of the front door. They were backlit and I had no idea who it was until Sam yelled, "Hey, Melanie! What are you doing here?" His voice was harsh and not at all friendly.

Just the question I would have asked. I kicked myself for not having secured the cottage as a secondary crime scene. But then, how could I have kept anyone away if they were really determined? Melanie came down the stairs, backpack over her shoulder, and said "Hi," but I noticed she avoided answering Sam's question.

"Can't stay," she said. "I've got a snake to follow."

We watched as she walked down the pathway to Stacey's cottage and out of sight.

"Where is her bike?" Sam asked.

Interesting question. Had she been sneaking about on foot, hoping to go unnoticed?

I looked back up at Stacey's cottage and wondered what her last few days had been like. What had happened to her that had led to murder?

"What happened in Stacey's last five days?" I said.

"Dunno."

"I thought she had the flu."

"That's what she said she had, but there was some other reason why she wanted to disappear for a while." He swung his backpack over one shoulder and had turned to go when I called him back.

I pulled his lab report out of my pocket and silently handed it to him.

"What were you analyzing when you got sugar?"

He took the piece of paper from me and scrutinized it for a long while, buying himself some time to respond.

"Just doodling around," he said. "Wanted to know if I could still remember the diagram for sugar."

Sam was a terrible liar. I snorted. He looked at me as if weighing his options.

"Okay. Okay," he said. "Stacey asked me to analyze something for her and I did. That's all."

"And you had no idea what you were analyzing?"

Sam looked at me as if to size me up and then said, "Look, she wanted it kept secret. Asked me not to tell anyone."

"But she is dead now. Surely she wouldn't mind if you told me, especially if it catches her killer."

Sam looked down at the ground and then back up at me. "It was Wyatt's vaccine." It took a bit of time to digest that.

"Wyatt's vaccine is sugar?"

Sam was fiddling with the strap of his backpack. "It's just a placebo. A useless fucking placebo."

chapter fourteen

S am dropped me off at the research station where
I hightailed it up to the mess for something to eat
for lunch. Everybody was long gone but there was still
some cold toast and warm milk. I helped myself and
went and sat at a table that, if the windows had not
been boarded up, would have overlooked the seaward
dunes. As I pulled back my chair I noticed some file
folders stacked on the chair beside mine. Someone
must have sat where I was sitting, dumped them on the
next chair while they were eating, and then forgotten
them. I reached over and picked them up — two in all.
They were personnel files stamped with OFFICE OF THE
DIRECTOR — Stacey. My interest was piqued. I picked
up the first of the folders and gave it a cursory look —
Melanie. There was a copy of her resume and a letter
offering her a research position at the station, along
with two photos, one black and white that had seen
better days and one colour that was dog-eared. In both

photos she looked out at the photographer with wary eyes, as if she was afraid her soul was being stolen, but there was something about the photos that made me wonder. The second folder was Sam's. As I was rifling through it I noticed there was a third file folder stuck inside as if by accident — Jayne's.

I thought I heard a door hinge squeak but when I looked up no one was there. I realized I was curious about who would come back for the folders and where they had got them. My guess was Darcy, since he had access to Stacey's files, but why would he be interested in these?

This time the squeak of the door resulted in someone being there. Not Darcy. Melanie. She stared straight at me, a look of confusion and what appeared to be annoyance flitting across her face.

I smiled at her. "Looking for these?" I asked and brandished the three folders at her.

She hesitated a moment and then said, "Pardon?"

I flapped the folders in her face. "Missing these?"

"What are they?" she said, remaining remarkably calm.

"I thought you might be able to tell me."

"I don't know what they are so how can I tell you?"

She was lying. I could tell by the set of her jaw and the fact that she refused to look me in the eye. Her glance veered off my left shoulder. I figured she and Sam were made for each other. They were both terrible liars.

"How did you get your research position here?"

She was taken off guard. "Stacey hired me."

"Did you know her?"

"Yes, but only by reputation."

"So you just applied and hoped for the best. After all, she must get hundreds of applications a year for these research positions. You were lucky."

"Not really. She came looking for me." Melanie said this with some pride, her hand flicking her blue hair out of her eyes.

"She came looking for you?" I realized it might sound like an insult so I added, "That's odd," which made it sound worse.

Melanie looked momentarily discomfited and I thought I saw fear in the look she gave me, but maybe not because she continued. "Stacey wanted someone with a solid research proposal and the ability to help around the station when needed. I had the best resume."

"But I thought you said —"

"Stacey got Darcy to ask me to submit my resume."

"But how did she know about you?"

Melanie looked away in confusion and, before I could pursue my line of questioning further, the screen door squeaked open and in popped Martha. When she spied me she headed in my direction and Melanie hastily retreated, but not before I caught her glancing furtively at the file folders. Had she filched them from Stacey's cottage?

"Hi there, stranger. You didn't come back and wake me up," said Martha in a slightly accusatory tone.

"I was otherwise occupied," I said.

Martha rolled her eyes, and then narrowed them as she pulled out a chair beside me. "Trevor said something about a fire at the lighthouse and that you were there."

"Trapped inside is more like it."

I told Martha all that had happened at the lighthouse without embellishing it too much but it didn't help. She still got upset.

"You mean you actually saw somebody slinking around the lighthouse?"

"No, but I heard them and I heard them drive away."

"Jesus, Cordi, you could have been killed."

But I shook my head. "I don't think so. The fire was set in a metal container and the only other wood was the door. The fire would have burned itself out before doing me any damage."

"But the vine could have broken."

"Yeah, that was a bit stupid. I should have just waited."

"So what are you saying?"

"That someone was trying to scare either me or Jayne."

"Jayne? What does she have to do with it?"

"I was on her ATV. You can't miss it with the big turtle painted on it. Someone could have mistaken me for her."

"Or not."

"There's that too," I said. "Someone could be trying to scare me off the case."

"You mean you're getting too close to something?"

"Yeah, but I don't know what. I mean I've discovered that Stacey and Jayne hate what Trevor does for a living and the massacre of turtles it causes."

I told Martha about Stacey being an observer and she and Jayne's fervent support of sea turtles.

"Trevor could have killed Stacey and he was in the area of the lighthouse when the fire broke out."

"What else?"

"There's something that happened around the time that Stacey became director and Jayne stepped down."

"Stacey was murdered for getting the job?"

"Oh c'mon, Martha," I said. "Who would murder for that?" But still — I found myself wondering the same thing.

Darcy interrupted Martha and me as we sat at the table. He folded his arms across his chest and leaned against the table.

"The police called. Said the earliest they could come was day after tomorrow."

"Really?" I said.

"Yeah I thought it was a bit late too, but they said the sea swells won't abate for a while and they are still busy with the devastation there. He says we're lucky the hurricane did an end run around us and blasted the mainland. Quite an opinionated guy he is. He said 'What's a barrier island useful for if it can't slow down a hurricane for the mainland?'" He smiled wryly.

"You could have told me that you didn't tell them we had moved Stacey," he added.

Oh boy.

"Detective Kennedy was very angry. It was after that that he said he couldn't come for a couple of days. *Contaminated crime scene* he called it. Made it sound as though it was no longer a priority. He would have preferred it if we had just let her rot. How callous is that?"

When I didn't say anything he said, "Just exactly what *did* you tell him?"

"What we knew at the time. That she'd been tied up and suffocated. He wasn't exactly paying close attention, what with the hurricane and all."

Darcy pushed himself away from the table and without looking me in the eye said, "I understand you got trapped in the lighthouse and someone lit a fire."

"She could have been killed!" said Martha.

"I doubt that," said Darcy, brushing off my escape like a fly, but I couldn't help notice that he had turned white. "Nothing to burn in that lighthouse, but why someone would want to torch the garbage defies reason."

"Cordi thinks it was someone after Jayne," said Martha.

Darcy's jaw dropped. "Are you saying you think this was deliberate?"

I started to answer but Martha jumped in. "We think it's a case of mistaken identity. That someone was after Jayne who lent her bike to Cordi."

Darcy looked as though he smelled a bad smell. "You can't be serious. Who would want to hurt Jayne?"

"Our question precisely," crowed Martha.

"While we're on this farfetched line of reasoning, maybe it was Cordi and someone was trying to scare her off looking for Stacey's killer," said Darcy.

Martha shrugged and I tried to look composed in the line of danger.

"On the off chance that such a spectacular theory is correct, I think you should stop snooping around," Darcy added.

"Cordi doesn't flinch at the first sign of danger." Martha pulled herself up to her full five feet of menace.

I glared at her but said nothing, which said everything.

Darcy was still standing by my side and I swivelled to look at him. "What do you know about the vaccine?" I asked.

Electrocution wouldn't have elicited as much of a response as my words did, but he recovered nicely. "What do you mean?

"I know it's sugar," I said and watched as the emotions on his face went from astonishment to fear to resignation.

"Sam," he said.

I nodded. I waited for him to regain his composure and then said, "How did Stacey know to test it?"

"I told her." He was going to make me work for every little bit of information.

"And what did you tell her?"

"I told her the vaccine was fake."

I was starting to get exasperated. "And why did you know that?"

Darcy unfolded his arms and ran a hand through his thinning hair. "I overheard Wyatt on the phone."

"And what did he say?"

"He was gloating about how the vaccine was fake and how much fun it was going to be when the first foal was born."

"He actually said that?"

Darcy nodded. "Yeah. He did."

"And what happened when you told Stacey?"

"I thought she'd go ballistic but she just smiled and asked me to steal a vial and get Sam to analyze it."

"Did she say what she was going to do with the information?"

"No." He said the word too strongly and emphatically. I looked at him but his face was blank and unreadable, and I thought maybe I was reading too much into it.

After Darcy left I picked up the third folder — Jayne's — and began opening it, but Martha was fidgeting so much beside me that I finally said, "What's the matter?"

She took a deep breath, glanced around to be sure we were alone, and then said, "I was really bored so I went exploring around the cabins while you were busy almost getting incinerated. I was within ten feet of the cabin that Rosemary and Melanie share when I heard a man's voice, low and angry. I was so startled at hearing a male voice that I kind of hung back in the palmetto. Prickly stuff that palmetto."

"Martha, you eavesdropped!"

"Well, what else was I supposed to do? Announce myself to them and get the hairy eyeball, or sneak away empty-handed?

"So what did you get?"

"The man was standing with his back to me, but I could tell by the white hair that it was Wyatt. He practically hissed at the other person in the cabin and said, 'How did you find out?'

"'Please Wyatt,' she answered. 'I won't tell. I know you had your reasons.' Her voice was pleading, tearful and scared and I knew it was Rosemary."

"And how do you know that? You some kind of clairvoyant?"

"She started to cry and it was quiet for a long time when I heard Wyatt whisper, 'It's okay, Rosemary, just as long as you don't tell. Because that would be a bad thing and you know how much I hate bad things.' His voice was unnerving."

Martha looked at me. "It was like menace wrapped in velvet. That's the only way to describe it." She paused and then continued. "Wyatt left the cabin then and I could hear Rosemary crying and it was all I could do not to go in and comfort her."

"I wonder if it's about the vaccine," I said.

"The fake one?"

"Yeah. Sam told me that the diagram on the paper I showed was from a vial of vaccine that Stacey gave him to analyze."

Martha let out a long low whistle. "But why wasn't Wyatt vaccinating the horses? Why was he giving them a placebo instead?"

"Maybe his services went to the highest bidder."

"You mean the islanders who were against the vaccination?"

I nodded.

"Does that mean Stacey stole the vaccine?" asked Martha.

"Seems weird to steal the vaccine and then announce it had been stolen. What was she trying to prove?"

"Maybe she had no choice. Wyatt complained. She had to act."

"What about which side of the debate she was on? Do we know that? If she was for the vaccination maybe Wyatt killed her to shut her up."

"I think Sam told me she was a devout Catholic, which, if logic prevails, would put her on the side opposing vaccination. After all, it is, by any other name, birth control."

"That would put her on Wyatt's side."

"Yeah, it would, wouldn't it?"

chapter fifteen

Martha was pushing a little pea around her plate when Sam walked in. He was soaking wet and I instinctively swivelled to look out the window, but of course I couldn't tell if it was raining because the windows were still boarded up.

He must have seen me because he grimaced and said, "Flooding down by the docks. I thought I could power through it but then my ride started coughing water halfway through and died right in the middle of the puddle."

He whisked a wet lock of hair out of his eyes and answered my question before I asked it. "I tried to pull it out but the footing was slippery. Had to hike over to the compound and get Trevor."

Trevor seemed to have his fingers in an awful lot of pies.

"Have you seen Melanie?" he asked as he glanced around the room.

I told him she had just been here and then I threw in a nice little aside. "Are you and she an item?"

Sam turned his head back to me, and the expression on his face told me he was wondering whether he should answer or not. "Let's just say we've been there, done that," he said. But there was no anger or even sadness, just frustration, which was kind of weird if they'd just broken up. Or maybe he was just frustrated with me.

"She seems like such a nice young woman," said Martha in an unbelievably matronly way.

"Yeah, well, people aren't always what they seem, are they?" he said bitterly.

The silence lengthened into the uncomfortable range, and I said, "Was Stacey?"

It was as if a fart had just been let loose.

"Was Stacey what?"

"Was she exactly what she seemed?"

Sam looked down at his feet and scratched his head. "Are any of us?" He looked at me with a steady gaze. "I don't know what you want, Cordi, but I will not speak ill of the dead. Stacey was a friend."

"But what if she was against the vaccination. The discovery that the vaccine was sugar would make her want to support the vaccination. You knew that and you couldn't let it happen so you killed her."

Sam looked at me, his mouth twitching in amusement. Finally he said, "You've got to be kidding. What kind of motive is that?" Said so baldly it did seem rather far-fetched.

I tried a different angle. "When exactly did Stacey discover that the vaccine was fake?"

Sam squared up his shoulders and brushed the hair from his eyes. I wondered why he didn't get sick of brushing the hair out of his eyes.

"When Darcy told her about the conversation he overheard with Wyatt."

"And when did you corroborate it?"

"I told her verbally the night before she announced someone had stolen the vaccine. She wanted the lab report and diagram to show to someone, but she didn't say who."

"How did she take the news?"

"She was visibly agitated but she was also in good spirits, as if she had just got a Christmas present she wasn't sure she deserved."

Someone dropped a pot in the kitchen and Sam jumped. I could see he was aching to leave. He kept looking up at the front door.

"Where were you when Stacey was killed?"

He glanced over at Martha. "I was with Martha until about 2:30 and then I went to bed, just like everybody else."

"Not quite everybody else," I said.

We stared at each other and then he abruptly said, "Gotta find Darcy. Be seeing you."

I watched as Sam threaded his way through the tables and out the front screen door, his bulk practically obliterating the doorway. Whatever was on his mind couldn't be anything compared to the physical damage he could do if he ever got angry. Had he got angry?

I had cabin fever and persuaded Martha to come with me to the beach. The sun was out but the wind in the upper canopy was still flag-flapping strong. It took us ten minutes to attach Martha's enormous bag to the back of the trike, and then Martha complained vociferously about getting onto my three wheeler, which required her to nearly do the splits. Once on she hung onto me so tightly I could hardly breathe. I wondered if maybe that was why they stopped making them, and not because if driven the wrong way they were major killers when they rolled over.

The trails were awash and several times we had to retreat from puddles that were too big and find another route. Even with the wind the interior of the island was soothingly quiet and sheltered by the dunes.

"What was all that about Mel anyway?" Martha yelled in my ear.

I pulled the trike over at the entrance to the beach and turned to look at her. She was so close I nearly hit her with my nose.

"Yeah, that was weird wasn't it?"

"They seemed as thick as thieves yesterday. What causes such a seismic change so quickly?"

"Murder?"

"You think they are involved somehow?"

"Sam can be pretty passionate."

"Passionate enough to kill because of three horses?"

"He knew the vaccine was fake and wouldn't work so, being on the side of habitat preservation, he would have wanted to make that public knowledge. Stacey, on the other hand, being on the side of God, would have wanted it to remain secret, so that the horses would breed before anyone was the wiser."

"That comes full circle, back to Sam murdering Stacey because of three horses."

It did sound pretty ridiculous.

"Maybe's he working on a higher plane. The greater good. The slippery slope. Vaccinate two horses and opponents will think you're opening the doors for an onslaught of vaccinations on millions of horses. He wanted to stop Stacey before she could do some harm.

"You really think someone would murder over fake vaccine?" asked Martha.

"Maybe Mel and Sam were in it together and one of them is getting cold feet."

"For heaven's sakes, Cordi, what motive could Melanie possibly have?"

"Maybe she doesn't have to have one. Maybe she helped him out because she loves him."

"And then she bails on him? I'm not buying it, Cordi. But if it's true that leaves two murderers who aren't talking to each other. A volatile situation."

I watched as Martha untied her bag and dragged it behind her down to the beach. It was a beautiful day but the wind was whipping sand in swirls around our feet. Martha sussed out a sheltered spot behind a dune and set up a blanket, pillow, towel, book, reading glasses, granola bars, potato chips, Kit Kat chocolate bar, water bottle, and suntan lotion. When she caught me staring at her she smiled and said. "You can share, Cordi."

What do you say to that? I smiled.

While Martha was staking out her spot I climbed the dunes to a point where I could see the entire length of the beach. It stretched from the north in a long band of dazzling white sand, swinging inland like a crescent moon and then swinging back, cradling the sea in its curve. A long row of pelicans braved the wind, flying as low to the water as they could, their gawky heads folded back upon their necks and their webbed feet tucked up close to their bodies. I came down off the dune and around to its backside and ground to a halt. Wyatt was sitting in meditation pose, eyes closed, his white hair as dazzling as the sand he sat on in the leeward of one of the dunes. I carefully backed away, not really wanting to talk to him.

"I won't bite, you know," he said through half-slitted eyes. How the hell had he known I was there?

I pretended I hadn't heard him and that he hadn't said anything.

"Nice spot for meditation."

He uncoiled his legs and bunched them up so that he was propping up his head on his knees.

"What brings you down here, Cordi?" and he flung out an arm to encompass the whole island.

"Research."

He smiled. Unnervingly inviting. "Research on what?"

"Bird song." He raised an eyebrow. "The dialects birds sing. Lots of birds sing the equivalent of English, cockney English, Scottish, Irish, Indian, depending on where they live. I'm just mapping it for the Indigo Bunting."

"Are you musical?"

I looked at him guardedly. "No. Not really."

"Sounds as though that would be quite challenging without a musical ear."

"It has its moments."

"But you plow right through them?"

"Something like that."

"Is something like that happening with Stacey's murder?"

I'd walked right into his trap and the only way out was to go on the offensive. "I know what you're hiding," I said.

A vein in his right temple twitched but the smile breaking across his face was at once warm and paternalistic. It momentarily took me off guard. "Do you now?" His smile didn't miss a beat.

"Your vaccine is fake."

I must hand it to him, he was as cool as they come. If anything the smile got broader. "So?"

"So, aren't there some ethical issues here?"

"Such as?"

"Such as lying to the islanders, taking their money, and doing the opposite of what you said you would do."

"Why do you think…?" He stopped suddenly, his smile fading.

"Lots of people would be ragingly angry to be so misled, if they knew," I said. When he didn't respond I continued, "Maybe Stacey found out about it. Threatened to expose you. So you killed her." *Much better motive than Sam's*, I thought.

He was smiling again. "I've got to hand it to you, Cordi. You are incredibly persistent, but you are way off base."

"Enlighten me then."

"I don't see you wearing a badge."

I ignored him. "Word leaks out that your vaccinations are placebos and your vet practice goes belly up. Stacey must have known that."

A shadow crossed his face and I knew I had hit a nerve.

"What was the note that Stacey gave you the night she died? Was it about the vaccine?"

Wyatt slowly rose to his feet, and as he walked past me he said, "You're way out of your depth, O'Callaghan."

It sent a shiver down my spine and I couldn't stop myself. Self-preservation I guess. "Do you really think that Stacey was the only one to know?"

There was a slight hesitation to his walk. "I'd be circumspect with that information if I were you," he said as he swivelled to face me.

"Is that a threat?"

"Just a piece of advice." And with that he turned and left.

chapter sixteen

With our backs to the sun we wended our way back through the forest, the trail stretching ahead like Hansel and Gretel's, the oak trees standing tall and proud, festooned with Spanish moss that hung from branches like Rapunzel's hair. I almost peered down to see if I could see the breadcrumbs.

As I veered around a stray branch that one of the wild old oaks had given up in the hurricane there was a loud bang, and an awful, jarring shudder ripped through my body. I immediately lost control of the trike, which leapt forward on altogether the wrong trajectory, tilting giddily on two wheels. I felt Martha lose her grip on me as I held on to the handlebars of a bike that was now airborne. I watched in fascination as the handlebars began to invert while gravity tore my body away from the bike. I landed on my back lengthwise in a ditch and watched helplessly as the trike turned over completely and then plummeted down on top of me. I held my breath and closed my eyes. There was a thud and then silence and a gentle pressure on my chest that felt like the weight of a wool blanket. I opened my eyes. The bike lay on top of me, straddling the ditch, its seat hung up on one side and the handlebars hung up on the other, with me underneath, pinned like an insect to a board. Couldn't even move my arms.

"Cordi! Cordi!" Martha was shrieking my name.

"Get me out of here!" I said, sympathizing even more with Duncan and the corner cupboard. All of a sudden Martha was right at my head, her frowning face peering into mine. She was covered in mud.

"You okay?" I asked. She nodded, her eyes wide and really startled looking.

"What the hell happened?" I said.

"Someone hit us from behind," said Martha, "but the sun was in my eyes so I couldn't see anything. I just flew off." She had a gnash over her left eye that was bleeding down her cheek.

"You sure you're okay?" I asked again.

She just stood there and nodded.

"Can you pull me out?" But she didn't seem to hear and I had to ask again. She pulled herself together and tried pulling me by my arms and then my legs but she wasn't strong enough to budge me.

"I'll be back, Cordi, with help," and she left me there to contemplate the vinyl seat of the trike and breathe in the gas fumes. I don't know how long I lay there before I heard the roar of an engine as it made its way toward me. I called out, thinking it might be someone other than Martha, and then wished I hadn't as I remembered Wyatt's last words to me. Was he out to get me? And if so was this him coming back? I held my breath and heard the engine die as someone called out. It didn't sound like Wyatt, so I answered. And suddenly there was Darcy at my side, making all kinds of are-you-ok sounds as I told him what had happened. He too tried to pull me out but when he started to try and shift the bike I yelled at him. It was a good way to crush me completely. So he stood around and waited with me, which I thought was really nice of him.

"I really think you need to take me seriously," he said.

"What do you mean?"

"Someone is trying to stop you from investigating this murder. This is the second time that you have had an inexplicable accident."

I felt a little chill go down my spine at the sound of inexplicable accident. Could someone have been after me? After all, Jayne wasn't a possible target this time.

Was I really a threat?

"I'm sure there is a logical explanation."

He looked at me and shook his head in frustration.

"What do you know about Melanie?" I asked, to take him off topic.

"Mel? Why do you ask?"

"She told me that Stacey sought her out. That she didn't apply herself for the job."

"That's right. Stacey's prerogative."

"Had she ever done that before?"

"Nope. Not that I know of."

"Any idea why she chose Melanie?"

"I think she saw something in her that reminded her of herself when she was young. Stacey was a bit of a romantic despite all her hard knocks and may have been trying to recreate her own life with a happier ending." I couldn't see his face but I could tell he was hiding something or making everything up as he went along.

By way of conversation I said, "That was pretty chilling finding Stacey like that. I can't get her out of my mind."

"I know what you mean."

"It's the slip knot that really gnaws at me."

"What do you mean?"

"You untied one hand. You must have seen how tight it was. She must have struggled something fierce trying to reach her mouth. What sort of sadist does that?"

"The chloroform would have taken care of that," he said.

I hadn't thought of that.

Darcy didn't say anything more and I strained my neck to see him. He was perched on a small rock just to my left and the look on his face was stricken with sadness, shock, and, if I was seeing him correctly, surprise. He obviously hadn't thought about it before and I was sorry for him that I had said anything.

I was never so glad to see Sam. He walked into my range of vision, looked down at me, and smiled. "Lucky lady," was all that he said as he reached under my shoulders and in one long fluid motion pulled me out from under the trike. Martha immediately rushed over and threw a blanket over my head and Wyatt, being a vet, had been commandeered to make sure I was all right because no one could find Duncan. Trevor and Darcy made up the rest of the rescue party and once I had been extricated they all put their hands to getting the trike back on the road.

Wyatt put his vet skills to work by politely asking if I was all right. When I said I was he wandered off in the direction of the trike. I looked behind them all and saw Trevor's truck. Martha saw me looking in its direction and said, "Do you think that's it?"

We went over to take a look but there was no telltale paint or bits of plastic sticking to it. In fact, the mud plastered all over it in a fine film was unscathed.

I looked up toward the trike as it coughed to life and saw Darcy staring at me. When he saw that I had seen him he quickly looked away. Could Darcy have run us off the road? It seemed unlikely, but he was in the area. I looked around for his vehicle but all I saw was the truck and the trike. Besides, any of the others could have been in the area too. They were certainly all close by because Martha hadn't been gone that long, even though it had felt as though she'd been gone a day.

Miraculously the trike was more or less undamaged, except that both the rear tires were flat. They lifted it into Trevor's truck and I watched as Martha opened the door and waved for me to get in. I was too wound up to get into that truck so I waved her off and told her to meet me at Stacey's cottage. What I needed was a brisk walk to vaporize all my demons. Darcy tried to get me to come with him but I said no and watched as they all left. I could hear the noise of their engines puttering through the trees, muffled like the pop of a cork. It was now a heavy, overcast day, the air practically molding its way around my body like a damp rag. I surveyed the trail in both directions and then struck out in the direction of the lighthouse and Stacey's cottage. I was kicking myself for not going sooner and wondered how many others had visited the cottage and pilfered some of Stacey's belongings. Had the murderer beaten me to a key piece of evidence? I cursed under my breath and quickened my pace.

Like all the cottages on the island, Stacey's stood at the base of the dune line and was built on stilts with the ubiquitous tower of stairs snaking up to the front door. I paused in the clearing and took it all in, the neat little shack where her ATV was stored and a pile of lumber by the stairs waiting for some project that she had had in mind, now but a lost dream. I started up the stairs two at a time but halted as my left leg gave out. I sat down on the stairs nursing it. I must have twisted it in the accident. As I sat there I heard a footfall above me. I turned to see Jayne coming out of the cottage. She had turned away from me and was backing up slowly, but it was too late and she knew it. She turned back and hailed me as if she hadn't tried to sneak away.

"Cordi. What are you doing here?"

"I could ask you the same question."

She laughed uncertainly and said, "Just looking for something I lent to Stacey." She started walking down the stairs toward me.

"You sound like Melanie. She was here looking for something too."

I stood up and turned to face her. "Seems she found what she was looking for," I said in a faintly accusatory tone of voice.

"I'm sure I don't know what you are talking about." Jayne reached my stair and stopped.

I made a giant leap of faith and said, "Three file folders. One with your name on it that maybe you are looking for." I wished to God I had read that third file folder but I wasn't going to let this chance go by.

"And why would I want my own file folder?" she asked.

"For the same reason anyone would. To read what people say about you. To assuage your ego. To still some fears. Or, in your case, to hide evidence in a murder investigation."

"Jesus, Cordi. Lighten up. What evidence could I possibly want to hide?" But her voice was wary.

When I didn't say anything she laughed. "You're just winging it, aren't you? Hoping I'll say something to incriminate myself. All I'll say is that Stacey and I agreed to disagree on just about everything but sea turtles. We were not friends but that is a lousy reason for killing someone." She passed me then on the stairs and I turned to watch her go. Without turning around she waved her hand and said, "Don't quit your day job, Cordi."

I was angry that I had boxed myself in. I shook the pain out of my leg and took the stairs two at a time, even though it still hurt. I pushed thoughts of Jayne out of my head and entered Stacey's cottage. There was an impressively huge picture window at the front of the house overlooking the canopy of trees. The main room was open concept with a long mahogany bar and a lovely maple island. Everything was burnt orange or pale yellow, from the sofas to the chairs to the burnt sienna walls, making it quite dark even with the picture window. I walked over to a bookcase lined not with books but with pictures. I scanned them for a while, looking for anything recognizable. I picked up one of a boy and a younger girl and peered at the faces. David was unmistakable — a little replica of his older self. The girl's face looked familiar but try as I might I couldn't see much of the young woman in the older Stacey. There were family photos too, but they were all from her distant past — nothing from Stacey's later life, as if she had just obliterated it. I wondered why and began to think about what Jayne had said: that something had happened to Stacey when she was young. What had happened to her that would wipe out her history from what must have been her late teens on?

There wasn't much upstairs other than the somewhat surprising find that she slept on a thin cot. The downstairs two bedrooms were sparsely furnished but both had double beds. The office was another story. It was in a large room that overlooked the snaking stairs outside. It was a riotous jumble of papers, computers, printers, photocopiers, file cabinets, two oversized desks, and an upholstered swivel chair that screamed out luxury. It was a daunting display of an academic at work, knowing no interruptions would occur. Of course, someone might just have ransacked the place. My heart plummeted at the thought, but then I started poking about and there was order to the mess. For whatever reason, Jayne and Melanie had been circumspect in their searches. I flipped through the filing cabinets — mostly personnel files and research projects. I set aside a file of newspaper clippings that, at a quick glance, related to a murder in Austin, Texas, hoping that what she had clipped randomly from newspapers might give me a clue. Next I rifled through some folders lying loose on her desk. Two were related to some of her research but the third was a correspondence file, which I set aside. And that's when I spied the yellow envelope, surely the one that I had seen David give to Stacey the day I arrived. Stacey's name was handwritten on the envelope and I carefully extracted the single sheet of paper from inside. It was a letter to Stacey from her doctor, saying he had tried to get in touch with her by phone with no luck and so was sending it via her brother. It was a gentle letter confirming a horrific blow. All the tests that had been done had excluded other causes. Stacey had had Lou Gehrig's disease.

chapter seventeen

I was sitting at the desk digesting this information when I heard someone starting up the outside stairs. I craned my neck to see who it was as Martha's curly mop of a head came into view. After several false starts she finally found me.

"Wheelchair heaven this is not," she said. "Do you realize I have not been to a single dwelling on this island that has fewer than seventy-five stairs?"

"Our cabins," I said, thinking what a nice warm feeling it is when someone else independently does the same thing as you; in this case counting stairs.

"Our cabins what?" she asked.

"Our cabins only have two stairs."

She rolled her eyes at me and asked what progress I was making.

"You remember when Darcy overheard Stacey and David arguing over a baseball player?"

Martha nodded.

"Well, it wasn't a baseball player. Well, actually it was, but it was also a baseball player's disease. Stacey had Lou Gehrig's disease."

Martha looked blank.

"It's a neurodegenerative disease — amyotrophic lateral sclerosis — that the baseball player Lou Gehrig had."

"Cripes. The one where you lose everything but your mind?"

"Yeah, that one."

"Her limp?"

"Would have been a symptom."

"How long did she have?"

"Her doctor said maybe two years at most, but miracles do happen. Look at Stephen Hawking."

"So her murderer could have just waited a few years and saved themselves the trouble."

"You could look at it that way," I said as something on the edge of my mind pulsed dimly and was gone.

"So anyone who knew about the disease is unlikely to be the murderer."

"Unless they murdered for money."

"Was she wealthy?" asked Martha.

"I don't know. Doesn't look like it." I glanced around the room and saw nothing of luxury, of expense, of overactive spending habits, except for the desk chair. This was the cottage of a woman who wasn't showing much of herself in her belongings other than what their absence said. Except for the photographs, of course.

Martha hung around for a while longer before she confessed to having a date with Duncan. When she told me she had a ride I handed her the files I had set aside and gave her Stacey's laptop to take back to the station. Since the cottage was already monumentally compromised I figured it would do no harm. After she left I booted up one of the two desktop computers Stacey had. After half an hour I was exhausted. There were so many files on so many different subjects with so many different names I was getting eye strain. It seemed to contain her entire life and I wondered what was on her laptop.

I was booting up her second computer when I heard a footfall upstairs, soft but unmistakable. I looked out the window at the snaking stairs wondering how I could have missed someone entering the cottage. There must be another entrance. I soft-shoed myself to the door and listened. There was no sound at all, not even a ticking clock. And then there it was again, a soft tread on the stair. I looked around wildly for some kind of weapon and blessed Stacey for being a romantic when I spied a five-pronged candelabra. I grabbed it with my right hand and raised it over my head as I stood behind the door. I listened to the footsteps padding slowly down the stairs and hitting the bare linoleum. *Definitely a man*, I thought as I gripped the candelabra more tightly. The footsteps turned away from me but some minutes later headed my way again. I stilled myself and as he came into view I tensed, ready to wallop him with my weapon. I was on a hair-trigger and just as I realized it was David my arm had started its downward trajectory onto his circlet of white hair. He yelped as he saw it coming and I managed to swing the candelabra clear of his head, but not before all the candles had tumbled down on top of him.

He had hit the floor in the classic arm over head pose of someone fending off a candelabra. I felt foolish until I realized that just because I knew him did not exclude him from my list of stalker suspects, so I kept a grip on the candelabra.

He looked up at me in astonishment. "What the hell was that all about?"

"I thought you were an intruder."

"Mother of God. You are the intruder. This is my sister's cottage. That candelabra should be in my hands. What are you doing here?"

I figured that if I told him I was looking for clues he'd freak out so I said, "I'm here to secure Stacey's office as a crime scene."

"As if anyone is going to be rifling through her things," he said dismissively.

"You're wrong there."

"Meaning?"

"Several people have already rifled through her things."

He narrowed his eyes. "Whatever for? There is nothing of value here."

I shrugged. "You sure of that?"

"What do you mean by that?"

"I assume you are Stacey's next of kin?" I said.

He nodded and then it dawned on him what I was getting at and he frowned. "Are you trying to imply that because I inherit from Stacey I am the murderer?"

Bingo! "All I am saying is that if Stacey was worth a lot of money you would definitely have a motive."

I couldn't read the look on his face — it was the face of a man just succeeding in hiding some powerful emotion.

"Are you named in her will?"

"She was my kid sister. I would never kill my sister." He spat it out in anger and I kept my silence. "She left what she had to me. I was all she had."

He turned to go but I called him back. "I found a medical letter in her belongings telling her she had Lou Gehrig's."

David stared at me and a little nerve twitched above his right eye. "What gives you the right to look through my sister's things?"

"Well, technically speaking, you did, among others."

"You take yourself too seriously, Cordi. You're not the police, you know."

"Don't you want to find out who killed your sister?"

"Of course I do." He rubbed his forehead with his hand and turned to look me in the eye. "Look, they gave her two years to live — two years of slowly losing everything. The cruelty of it is that the mind is left intact to witness the awful deterioration of the body."

"Couldn't have been easy for her."

David laughed. "My but you have a way with words. Of course it wasn't easy, the tentative diagnosis came last month but they had to do tests to be sure. That letter you read was just confirming the worst. From the moment she knew, she hid it, maybe even from herself, but I wouldn't know because she wouldn't talk to me."

"You weren't close." I stated it as a fact not a question.

"We were once —" he started, then stopped abruptly.

"What happened?" I asked.

He looked at me through narrowed eyes again and said, "You ask too many personal questions, Cordi. Most people don't like that." Said that way it sent a shiver down my spine.

"When I first met you, you called the biologists here dedicated," I said. He glanced up as if wondering where I was going. "You also said they weren't harmless. Care to elaborate?"

He laughed an empty laugh. "If you're looking for demons, most of them are guilty of one thing. They just couldn't accept how big she was. She was a decided anomaly among biologists the world over. They never let her fit in."

"Maybe she didn't want to fit in?"

"Really, Cordi. Can you name one person who doesn't want to fit in and be part of things?" The question lingered between us for a while. "She wasn't always fat you know."

I waited.

"When she was eighteen she just started eating and eating and she couldn't seem to stop."

"What happened to her?" I held my breath.

We were still standing over the upended candelabra when he suddenly walked toward the desk and began searching for something, my question discarded like a used match.

In my most authoritative voice I said, "This is a crime scene. You can't do that."

"Where's her laptop?" he asked, ignoring my demand.

"It's been impounded," I said.

"Impounded where?" He rubbed his eyes with his hand. He was getting impatient and I didn't know why. "For god's sake there's nowhere on this island to impound anything. May I remind you once again that you are not the police?"

"I sent her computer back to the station so that nobody could surf through it."

"What's wrong with leaving it here?"

I hesitated. Had he forgotten? "Because several people have been here before you, looking for I know not what. I just thought it wise to secure her laptop."

"Who's been here?" he asked.

I ignored him and said, "What do you want with her laptop?"

"I have to make funeral arrangements. She kept that sort of stuff on her laptop."

"You mean her will."

"Well, actually you don't usually put your funeral requests in your will, but a copy of it would be there too." He stiffened, as if he'd said too much, and then he bent over and picked up the candelabra. "After all these years the fool kept this," he said under his breath and traced a hand along a dent in one of the arms. Then he caught himself and turned to look at me. "She had a hard life." With that he walked out the door.

I hung around a little while longer but I was keen on getting back and looking at Jayne's file folder and Stacey's laptop. Something told me that they would give me more pieces to the puzzle.

The sun was still high in the sky when I sealed Stacey's door with masking tape — kind of useless — and headed down the stairs. I decided to bushwhack through the live oak and palmetto to the beach. It was tough slogging, the palmetto kept grabbing at my clothes and the bugs were really bad. I smelled the sea before I saw it, that pungent aroma of seaweed and salt, sun and wet sand. I hadn't taken more than a step toward the dunes when someone yelled, "Stop! Don't move!" The voice was loud and insistent. I stopped.

The voice came from somewhere behind me and to my right. "Do not move a muscle," it said.

"What's wrong?" I asked in alarm.

"There is a rattlesnake two feet from your right foot. Don't look! I'm going to approach it from behind and use some tongs to capture it. Stay put."

I watched as Melanie slowly came into my line of vision as she skirted me and came in behind the rattler. She was carrying a long metal rod with tongs on one end and a handle to control them on the other. She moved very slowly into position and I was dying of an itchy nose. The rattler was coiled in a lovely cone with the tip of its tail poking up next to its unblinking eyes. Surely I was far enough away to just make a dive for it but Melanie was in charge. I watched as she grasped the snake behind its neck as it lashed out. I itched my nose and backed away. She disappeared behind a dune and when she didn't return after two minutes I started toward it. She had all her gear spread out and I realized with dismay that I had interrupted her research.

"Sorry," I said.

She looked up at me. She was wearing mosquito netting and I couldn't really see her face. "It's okay, I guess. Just frustrating. I've just spent three hours watching this particular snake — I don't have the money for transmitters and the snakes are not easy to find."

I said sorry again. I had just blithely broken both of Stacey's cardinal rules. Melanie stood up and took off her mosquito hat. I must have looked dumbfounded because she took a step backwards and said, "What's wrong?"

I wasn't quite sure how to put it. A thousand thoughts were chasing through my mind as I put two and two together and actually got four.

"I just saw a picture of Stacey when she was a young girl."

Melanie breathed in.

"She looks exactly like you."

Melanie didn't say anything. She just stared at me.

I took a chance. "When did you know?" I asked.

"Know what?" said Melanie. She had regained some of her composure, but she was on the defensive — like a boxer just barely holding her ground, waiting.

"That you have to be Stacey's daughter."

Melanie coughed and flicked the blue hair out of eyes that looked hunted, haunted, and trapped. "What business is that of yours?" she said defiantly.

I didn't say anything and the silence grew. Finally I said, "You know you can't hide it. I already know your secret. So when did you find out?"

I watched as her eyes found a way out of their trap and she made her decision. "About two months ago, shortly after I applied for the research position."

"And Stacey hired you."

She hesitated, still grappling with some inner demons. "That's right," she finally said. "The Island Association wanted someone to do some research on rattlesnakes and copperheads. It was pretty fierce competition so I was really excited when I got it. I was so proud of myself. I actually thought I got the position with no pull." She looked at me then, a forced smile on her face and her eyes blank.

"But Stacey saw your application photograph ..." I gently prodded.

"Yeah. She saw my photograph and realized I was her daughter." Melanie sighed and stood up. "I was on the island a month before she told me."

"What did she tell you?"

"That she got pregnant when she was eighteen years old and gave me up for adoption. The usual story, isn't it? Get loved. Get laid. Get rid of baby." The bitterness in her voice was palpable.

"I take it you didn't exactly get along."

"Not at first. I mean, would you? She just abandoned me." She said it as if by rote, or perhaps she was simply disassociating herself from the trauma in some way.

"Maybe she had her reasons."

"Yeah, that's what they all say." She pitched her voice mockingly high and angry and said, "I was too young and I couldn't take care of you. I had no choice. You're better off with someone else. Did she ever stop to think that the someone else might be worse?" Challenging words that she had obviously spoken before. Melanie stared at me, daring me to speak, waiting for an answer I could not give.

She shrugged, her voice softening. "Water under the bridge now."

She was about to continue when she looked over my shoulder and slowly began to smile. I turned to look and saw Duncan skirting the dune like a man on reconnaissance.

"It's okay, Duncan," Melanie called out. "I'm not doing any studies." Which made me feel guilty as hell, having literally blundered into her study site. Stacey would not have been amused.

I watched Duncan morph back into an ordinary man as he came to join us. He clamped his large hand on Melanie's shoulder like an old friend and I looked at him quizzically.

"Mel and I are old friends," he said. "We go back two whole months."

Mel smiled. "Duncan found a rattler in his cottage

shed and came to find 'the new snake girl.' I've since logged many hours on that snake. Duncan helped me tag him with a nonpermanent marker."

The three of us stood there shuffling our feet until Duncan said, "Was I interrupting something?"

Melanie looked at me quickly with an almost imperceptible shake of the head.

"No, no were just talking snakes," I said. It was awkward, not really knowing what Melanie wanted, so I added, "Let me know if you ever find a copperhead. I'd really like to see one," and I left them conversing about Sebastien — presumably the snake in Duncan's garage. I broke out of the dunes onto the beach and strolled along the water's edge. There wasn't a soul in sight. I took my running shoes off and walked through the surf, the wind chasing my hair all over my face. I was lost in thought when, from somewhere behind me, I heard my name called. Duncan.

I turned and watched him labouring toward me. He's a big man and the loose sand just seemed to hold him back at every step. He finally changed course so that he was walking on the wet sand that the tide had fashioned into something as hard as tarmac. In fact, I had been told that at low tide planes could land on the beach.

We walked companionably in silence until Duncan turned and said, "How goes the investigation?"

I grimaced. "It's all over the map. There are so many loose ends that I'm not sure there are any attached ends."

"I was just talking to Martha. She says you nearly had another very serious accident."

"Yeah. Well …" was all I could say.

"You think it was Darcy? Martha said he was the first on the scene."

"It could have been Darcy but then why would he do such a thing?"

"He doesn't want you to continue the investigation for some reason?"

"He's certainly made no bones about that. But he says it's because of my safety."

"And maybe it is. Who else was there?"

"Wyatt, Sam, Trevor — they all came together except Sam. Any of them could have done it."

"Someone feels threatened, and since you didn't know any of these people until you came here two days ago it has to have something to do with your investigation." We walked some more in silence.

"I am no closer to finding out who did it. I haven't even been able to eliminate anybody." Duncan gave a snide little snort and I laughed. "Not that kind of elimination," I said.

"Surely my little Melanie is no murderer," said Duncan with a smile that faded quickly once he saw the look on my face. "What? What is it?"

Melanie hadn't specifically asked me not to tell and I needed a sounding board so I said, "Stacey was Melanie's mother."

Duncan stopped dead in his tracks and grabbed me by the shoulders. "What? You have got to be kidding."

I shook my head and he let go of my shoulders.

"Melanie is Stacey's daughter. They hid it well."

We began to walk again and after half a football field of silence I said, "Melanie only found out about it once she got to the island. She was very bitter. Felt she'd been abandoned by a selfish teenager."

"A selfish and lost teenager."

"She doesn't see it that way. At least, I don't think she does. Do you know anything about Melanie's life?"

"Only that she was in and out of foster homes and is a sort of miracle child for making something of her life."

"There was real anger there Duncan."

"I hear you, Cordi, but I don't want to believe she is capable of murder."

"She blames her mother for a lousy childhood. It's a motive."

"But there are others who could have done it too, right?"

"Yeah, Sam has a wishy-washy motive. He and Stacey could have argued over the vaccine. And Trevor could have done it because of her stance on conservation. I haven't been able to come up with any motives for the rest yet, but I'm working on it."

"That's what worries me. You're maybe working on it too hard. What if whoever it is succeeds next time?"

"Well, I'm not about to make a public announcement that I'm quitting. I'm not a quitter."

"Even with your life at stake? You could pretend to quit."

"Listen to yourself, Duncan. How do I pretend to quit and then continue to investigate? The first person I question would blow the whistle. I'll just have to be careful, that's all."

More silence and then, "What's this about Lou Gehrig's disease?"

"Pretty awful, isn't it? She was so alone with such an awful prognosis."

"It may be an awful thing to say but perhaps there was some luck in her murder. She'd be spared all that agony."

"Is death ever preferable to life?" I asked.

"Sometimes it is, Cordi. Sometimes it is."

chapter eighteen

I finally made it back to my cabin. There was no sign of
Martha but Stacey's laptop was plunked down on top of
my bed. I pushed it aside and rummaged around the sheets
for the file folders. I pulled them out and Mel's folder
slipped and sprawled all over the floor. I picked up the
colour photo of her and then looked more carefully at the
older black-and-white one. Had I been thinking I would
have recognized that it was old, way older than Melanie.
The resemblance really was quite striking and I marvelled
at how often the puzzle of life threw parents offspring who
were their spitting image. Of all the combinations and per-
mutations of DNA, eggs, and sperm, that happened more
often than one would expect. I thought about Duncan
and his gargantuan nose and I wondered if all his children
would have been so cursed, had he had kids. And then I
wondered if that was why he hadn't had kids.

I dropped Melanie's folder on the floor and picked up
Sam's. Last name Jamieson. He was a Georgia boy, born,

raised, and educated in Athens. Not much else in his file. I turned to Jayne's. The mandatory picture and application form stared up at me and I looked at it in surprise. Gertrude Jayne. Gertrude. No wonder she had clung to Jayne. I picked up Sam's folder again. Someone had obviously misfiled her folder into Jamieson. Maybe Melanie hadn't even known it was there and maybe that's what Jayne had been looking for. Jayne had been director for seven years and, according to her file, they had all been good until her last six months when the paper trail ended.

She had a Ph.D. from a small Midwestern university, and by the looks of it had published a lot of papers on sea turtles. *Nothing here*, I thought, and was about to close the folder when a piece of paper caught my eye. It was stuck to the last sheet in the folder and I slowly pried it free. It was a photocopy of Jayne's Ph.D. degree that had been faxed to the recipient, whoever that was. Stuck to the degree was a little stickum with the email address for Nebraska State University. The degree said she had graduated in 1990 summa cum laude. I chewed that over for a while, wondering why I was paying it much attention, until I heard a commotion in the next cabin over. I unashamedly moved to the open window and eavesdropped.

I could see Rosemary through the open window in the other cabin. She was holding her head and telling someone to leave her alone.

"How can I leave you alone?" Wyatt came into view, walked up behind her, and put his hands on her shoulders. She flinched. I had the flight-or-fight reaction to that. Would I have to go to her rescue? But what he said next stopped me in my tracks.

"You're telling people I'm beating you," he said, his voice dangerously level. "Why would you do that?"

I held my breath.

"You scare me."

"I thought we were colleagues. Friends."

"We were friends. We are friends. And I didn't really tell anyone. They just jumped to conclusions. I have no control over that."

"Well la-di-da. No control, eh? You could do the decent thing and deny it."

"I did. I have."

"Not bloody hard enough." He hesitated and then said, "You're fired, my friend, so get the hell off this island before I do something you'll regret." He moved out of sight to appear on the front porch. He paused there a moment, as if he was going to go back in, but he didn't. Instead he slammed the door and left.

An hour later and I was deeply immersed in Stacey's laptop, which was a treasure trove of everything I didn't really need to know, until I located a folder buried inside a folder. It was labelled *News Clippings*. There were twenty-five to thirty files. I started with the first one and by the time I got to nineteen I was practically comatose from all the random clippings. I fervently hoped I would not have to do this all again on her desktop at the cottage. Then I opened number twenty and nearly dropped dead.

It was a picture of an ecstatic Stacey, her smile threatening to obliterate her face. She was holding an enormous cheque and my heart stopped when I read the amount: forty-one million dollars. Canada's newest lottery winner. I checked the day. Five years ago. I was sitting there, thinking about all the implications, when Martha arrived with a thump of the door and a deep sigh.

I looked up.

"Don't ask," she said and then she told me anyway. "I went swimming in the tidal creek between the two islands but nobody told me there's one hell of a riptide when the tide's going out. Anyway it ripped off my bathing suit and there I was in my altogethers trying to figure out how to get my towel without anyone seeing me."

I tried not to smile.

"I had to crawl out and along the beach. I felt like a regular G.I. Joe."

I lost the battle and started to laugh. "God, Martha, didn't you remember about the spaniel? What made you decide to go swimming at all? The seas are still horrendous."

"I was hot and the creek looked benign. What can I say?"

She plunked herself down on the bed and eyeballed the laptop. "So?" she said.

I looked at her and smiled, relishing what I was going to say next. "Stacey is worth more than *forty-one million dollars*."

Martha's jaw dropped. "Jesus. I never saw that coming."

"Neither did I."

"So who gets it all?"

"David says he does," I said.

"But you are not so sure?"

"No. I mean how does he know? Did she tell him? They weren't exactly talking to each other."

"With that kind of money there's got to be a will. What about the laptop? Maybe there's a copy there."

I couldn't believe I hadn't thought of that myself. I picked up the laptop and keyed in the search term *will*. A lot of garbage items came up, with the word *will* somewhere in them. Three looked promising but I came up empty handed. Two were templates for wills and the third was a diet labelled *Willpower*.

"Try testament," said Martha.

"Oh come on, who would use that antiquated term?"

"Someone wanting to hide it without resorting to a password."

"I'll be damned," I said.

There were two, one dated a month ago the other a year ago. I chose the will with the latest date and opened it. Martha came over, stationed herself behind my left shoulder, and we began to read it together.

"Jesus, Cordi, stop itching."

I hadn't realized I had been itching but once she brought my attention to it the itches suddenly came into stark relief. All over my lower legs and up to my waist. *Must be the laundry detergent I'm using here*, I thought, and tried to shove it out of my mind.

"Looks like David doesn't get it all," muttered Martha as she brought me back to the business at hand. "But why would Melanie get forty-seven percent? By all accounts they hardly knew each other."

I realized that Martha didn't know — I was losing track of whom I'd told and whom I hadn't.

"They may not have known each other but they were blood relatives," I said.

Martha looked stunned.

"She was Stacey's daughter." I must say it felt good imparting such startling news and I watched Martha's face as it roller coastered through her emotions, from initial disinterest to stunned disbelief to a realization of what the information meant.

"Forty-seven percent of forty-one million dollars is a multimillion dollar motive," she said.

"And fifty percent isn't a bad take on David's part either," I said. "Money that big can kill multiple times."

"And Darcy gets three percent, well over a million dollars, which seems paltry in the rarefied company of Melanie and Wyatt."

"Yeah, but it's enough to give a young man a good motive," I said as I used extraordinary willpower to stop from scratching my legs.

"What's the old will say?" asked Martha.

I opened the document and we glanced through the will. David had been right a year ago. He got it all then.

"So Melanie wasn't on Stacey's radar a year ago," I said.

"Doesn't look like it."

"We have Melanie, Darcy, and David with a money motive, Sam who we think disagreed with Stacey over the vaccine, Trevor whose kids went hungry because of all the rules to conserve the turtles."

"What about Wyatt?" said Martha. "He stood to lose his reputation and his vet practice if Stacey had exposed him."

"So he kills her because of the fake vaccine?"

"Or maybe she was blackmailing him and he'd had enough." I started itching again. It felt as though I was being tickled by a thousand feathers.

"And then there's Jayne," I said, trying to ignore the itches. "I don't know why but there's something there."

"What do you mean?"

"She's hiding something. I just know it," I said, as I finally gave in to my itches full throttle.

"Jesus, Cordi. What's with the itching? You're driving me crazy."

I could have said the same about the itching.

"What about Rosemary?" asked Martha.

"I don't know about Rosemary. She's an enigma."

I told Martha what I had overheard between Rosemary and Wyatt.

"Why would she want to let us jump to conclusions?" asked Martha.

"More to the point, why did she say she had denied it when she definitely hadn't? At least not to me. Makes you wonder what else she might be lying about."

Martha looked at me, threw her arms up in the air and said, "Everybody has a motive. Nobody has an alibi. Somebody is a murderer."

The sun was heading toward the horizon when I took a break from all the newspaper clippings and lottery winnings and left Martha poring over Stacey's computer. The itching was driving me as crazy as Martha had implied it was driving her. Only she didn't have to wrestle with the little stabbing pinpricks the way I did. I was beginning to wonder if any allergy to detergent could cause such intense itching. I needed to clear my head so I walked down to the beach and watched the sun set amidst some angry swirling clouds. I walked a long time, as night fell. There was no moon and the only light was the cresting waves in the tattered starlight. I walked along the hard-packed sand of the beach toward the tidal creek, the warm wind from the sea washing over me, as timeless as it was constant. This place really had me thinking of eternity, I guess because it reeked of remnants of a distant age.

I was thinking about turning around and heading back for something to eat when I heard the roar of an ATV. I turned and saw its headlights coming closer and closer to me. I waited, expecting it to slow down, but it quickly gained speed and was heading right for me. I waved my arms and yelled but it didn't stop and I started running, zigging and zagging my way across the beach. It couldn't turn on a dime the way I could, but whoever was driving it was good. I sprinted toward the tidal creek and hesitated only a fraction of a second before doing a shallow racing dive into the water. It was strangely warm and enveloping and I treaded water as I looked back to see the ATV poised on the bank, its headlights blinding me to who was driving. Then the headlights turned and the ATV disappeared and I was left behind in the darkness. Suddenly I felt the strength of the current take me, like a punch in the gut, and haul me out to sea. I tried to swim ashore but it was too strong. I finally remembered the spaniel and the sandbar he had ended up on with the young boy. Should I stop fighting the current and trust that I'd be deposited on the sandbar or did I continue to fight to get ashore? But my attempts were futile and I realized if the sandbar wasn't there, there was nothing between me and the open sea.

The current carried me for what felt like ten hours but must have only been a couple of minutes before my right leg brushed against what I sure hoped was sand. The sandbar was just above sea level, but it was there, and I crawled up on it and rested. I was there a long time, long enough for the tide to turn and start coming in, nibbling away at my sandbar as it did so. I stood up and surveyed my situation. Although it was dark I could still see the main beach and the water in between. The sandbar was about one hundred yards out from the beach, the water between me and shore looked calm, and the tide was with me this time. I was just about to wade in when something broke the surface of the water, its triangular fin glistening in the starlight. I tried to remember my porpoise and shark fins but there was no way for me to identify the owner of the fin. I stood there paralyzed as the water swirled in around me, obliterating my sandbar. I had no choice. I had to swim for shore. I psyched myself up, then dived in and swam like a maniac, agonizingly aware that sharks feed on frenzy, dreading the serrated teeth on my leg, my stomach, my head, forcing myself to swim through the dread until, miraculously, my hand hit shore and I scrambled up the beach, a roiling mass of nerves, to lie prostrate on the cold wet sands of safety.

I lay there until I started to get cold and then I ran back to the station to try and warm up and banish the shark-infested demons of my mind. Fortunately Martha wasn't in the cabin so I was able to change out of my wet clothes without her haranguing me. *As she had a right to do*, I thought. Whoever had been driving that ATV would have had a good view of me. No mistaken identity here. I went and took a shower because the itching was so bad I couldn't stop. In the shower I looked aghast at the welts all over my lower legs and around the area of my waistband and crotch. This was no laundry detergent. This had to be an insect or something. The only thing that came close on the scale of itch factor was spider bites that itch and itch and linger and linger. But there were way too many bites for even multiple spiders and I couldn't see anything crawling on me.

My stomach was growling up a storm and I went in search of something to feed it. There was no one in the clearing. I climbed the steps to the mess, walked in, and went to the kitchen, snuffling around the fridge to see if there was anything edible at all.

I was reaching for an apple when I heard a man cry out, "God damn it. You owe me big time. How many people know it's fake?"

"Settle down. Settle down. We can't talk here."

"Dammed right we can talk here." Trevor was pale faced and shaking.

The other person was out of sight but I was pretty sure I knew the voice. Wyatt.

"We had a deal. You blew it. You owe me," said Trevor.

"Extenuating circumstances. How was I to know that she would interfere and screw it all up?"

"We had a deal. I want my money back." Trevor slammed his hand on one of the tables. "I won't let you off this island before you pay me."

"Don't make empty threats. There are others who know how to drive a boat, you idiot."

"Just watch me," said Trevor and he turned and walked out the door, slamming it behind him.

My hand was still reaching for the apple when I heard a sharp intake of breath. I turned and there was Wyatt, staring at me, sort of like the snake had hours earlier.

"How long have you been here?" His voice was sharp, gruff, and angry.

"Long enough."

He didn't say anything and looked unsure of himself, which must have been an anathema to him.

"You got paid to doctor the vaccine," I said.

He just stared at me.

"But the islanders voted for a real vaccine."

"You can't always get what you want." He sang the words in a rich bass voice that sounded nothing like his real voice and took me off guard. I'm a sucker for a bass voice.

I recollected myself and said, "You got paid twice."

He laughed. "You didn't hear it from me."

"I guess not. It would not be in your interests to broadcast your behaviour, would it?"

When he didn't answer I said, "You'll lose your licence. Your livelihood."

He snorted. "You think there aren't other fish in the sea? This is just one of many stops along my route. I couldn't give a damn."

But just in case he could give a damn and acted on it I said, "Your secret's out. I'm not the only one who knows it."

He smiled then, a slow Cheshire cat kind of smile that gave me the creeps. "You're very transparent, O'Callaghan, and repetitive I might add. Do you really think I'd try to kill you to preserve my secret?"

I didn't want to answer that so instead I sent another salvo over his bow. "Why do you beat Rosemary?" I wanted to startle him out of his side of the story.

"I don't," he said, before he caught himself. "What business is it of yours whether I do or not?"

"It should be everybody's business if you are beating her, but if you aren't why is she saying you are?"

He glared at me. "Because she's a bitch." That was not very enlightening.

"Are you sleeping with her?"

"She's my assistant, for god's sake. Why would I stoop so low as to sleep with my assistant?"

"Oh, come on. A pretty young girl."

"She's not my type," he said harshly.

"That sounds like it means she has some kind of power over you."

"You have a pretty poor opinion of me if you think I just jump every woman I meet. You hardly know me. Where is this coming from?"

"You're good-looking and in a position of power. She's pretty. It's hard to believe you're not sleeping together."

"You have a pretty poor opinion of her too. She's a big girl. Whatever happened to freewill and feminism? I'm not her master."

"So she said no to you?"

He stared at me, unblinking.

"She knew about the vaccine."

He just kept staring.

"She was blackmailing you."

How can a man not blink for so long? It was unnerving.

"Was Stacey blackmailing you too?"

"This conversation is over," he said and turned on his heel, leaving me standing there, wondering.

chapter nineteen

I made sure Wyatt was long gone before I went snooping through the research station. Unlike the dining room, which was homey and decorated with art and nice furniture, the rest of the station was by-the-book research labs and offices, all basically the same layout — a rectangle. What was in them made them unique. The first one was full of glass jars filled with formaldehyde and various creatures of myriad description lining an entire wall. I slowly scanned each bottle as I walked the length of the room. There were bottled baby sea turtles in different stages of growth, fish of various sorts, and even a baby feral pig. I turned away from this litany of horrors and looked at the rest of the room. There were two desks, one neat, one messy, a couple of bookshelves, and three aquaria. I headed over to take a better look and jumped back as something in one of the terraria jumped out at me. Fortunately the glass was in the way, and I looked with interest at a young and very poisonous copperhead snake. It was slithering along the ground of the terrarium and the sun streaming through the window caught and held the corn-coloured head and black mask. But it was the eyes that were mesmerizing. Golden with a jet-black vertical slit of a pupil. I could understand why such eyes might freeze prey. And why the term *snakelike* had such bad connotations. Still, it was quite beautiful and I wondered if I would still think it beautiful minus the danger it posed. Perhaps the danger heightened the beauty?

A cricket chirruped nearby and I looked around for the source — a small box with a holey lid. When I peered inside I could see about three-dozen crickets milling about. Food for the snake, I figured.

I was checking out the anoles in one of the other two terraria when Sam walked in and stopped uncertainly when he saw me.

"I was just looking for Mel," he said in a voice that made me think otherwise.

"So this is Mel's lab?" I asked, trying not to scratch.

"Yeah, Mel and Charlie."

"Who is Charlie?"

"Her supervisor. But he's hardly ever here. He gets Mel to do all the work."

"Are you and Mel back together again?" I asked, as an itch surfaced in agonizing fashion and had to be scratched.

He was hovering near the door looking very uncomfortable and I got the impression he just wanted to turn tail and leave. But he didn't.

"No," he said, showing no emotion at all.

I didn't say anything, hoping he'd traipse through his own silence. And he did. "She has some of my lab gear that I want back," he said. He looked over at what was presumably her desk — the messy one — and I saw a pained look cross his face as he brushed his eyes with his hand.

"Did she leave you?"

He jumped as if I'd hit him. Nope.

Next thought. "Why did you leave her?"

He squared up his considerable shoulders and said, "What would make you think that?"

"Because of something that you intimated to me: that Melanie was not what she seemed."

A look of surprise and anger flitted through his face. "I don't see that that's any of your business," he said, but there was no bite to his words.

"You know, don't you?"

"Know what?"

"That Melanie was Stacey's daughter."

Sam stood stock-still and I could hear the crickets chirruping as he weighed this information. There was no surprise on his face but there was indecision and maybe a little bit of fear.

Finally he nodded and said, "She told me, but she made me promise not to tell anyone. She and Stacey wanted their privacy. I respected that."

"And that's why you broke off with her?"

Sam abruptly moved over to Mel's desk and began rummaging around. "She said my compass was here somewhere." His voice trailed off. He sounded like a lost little boy and I wondered why he felt lost if he was the one to break it off. But he wasn't saying.

I couldn't stand it any longer and when I thought his back was to me I itched my legs, my stomach, my crotch in a mad dash effort to kill the itches.

"I see you've got chiggers," he said, obviously having a hard time not smiling.

"Chiggers?"

"Have you been bushwhacking?"

I nodded, remembering my wade through the palmetto.

"Yup. Chiggers."

"Which are?"

"You haven't heard of them?" he said incredulously. "Must be just a southern thing."

"So what are they?" I asked impatiently.

"They belong to the spider family and are related to mites. It's the larval form that does all the damage."

"But I have dozens of bites and I haven't seen a single one."

"And you won't. They are microscopic."

"Oh my God. Like no-see-ums." And I suddenly felt them scrambling all over me and resisted the very strong urge to run screaming from the room.

Early the next morning I was getting station fever and the itching wasn't helping. I needed a break so I went and revved up my trike, with two fresh new tires, and did a wheelie out of the clearing as I veered to avoid someone racing in. I slowed down enough to catch a glimpse of Darcy and the hand he waved at me.

The back roads were peaceful and all the hectic details of the investigation just slipped away as I drove through that tunnel of trees with the Spanish moss weighing down the branches. I stopped for a while to let an armadillo cross the needle-covered road and then just let the trike take me where it felt like going. After half an hour of wandering the pathways I found myself at the compound where the ferry left for the mainland. This was Trevor's territory.

I got off the trike and began exploring, hoping to find Trevor somewhere among all the buildings. Actually there were just three — two large tin semicircles and one square tin — all remarkably ugly. In fact, the whole compound was as ugly as I remembered it, with all manner of vehicles in various stages of repair strewn around, along with building materials, boats, and cement blocks. I wandered down toward the water and, for the first time, noticed a house tucked into a grove of trees so that it was almost completely hidden. I looked more closely, saw Trevor's truck pulled up outside, and realized this was where he must live.

I put my hand on the hood of the truck — still warm, so he had only just come home. In an instant I made up my mind and strode down the stone walkway to the house and rang the bell. I had a moment of the heebie-jeebies as I realized how deserted this place was, but he answered the door immediately and I had to think of something to say. Which I couldn't — *Hi, I was just in the neighbourhood and stopped to say hello* just didn't sound right so we stood and looked at each other for a while until he said, "Hello, Cordi. What can I do for you?"

"I just wanted to ask you some questions. It won't take long."

He opened the door wider. "You'd better come in then. I've got something on the stove."

Inside was a huge and very dark living room and every inch of every wall was filled with a clock of some description — many of them cuckoo clocks that made me wonder how he slept at night. Did they all keep exactly the same time and go off altogether or were they staggered so that every hour the chiming lasted five minutes or more. I tore my eyes from his clocks and saw that despite the darkness there was a large bay window overlooking a deck and beyond that the tidal creek.

He disappeared into what was presumably the kitchen and I heard him rummaging around. I walked over to a pine sideboard that appeared to be homemade and looked at some of the pictures. One stood out. It was a family photo of Trevor and what must have been his wife and their blond curly headed daughter, looking through the mesh of a shrimp net. Trevor had both his arms wrapped around his wife and daughter and his smile was infectious.

"That was taken on my shrimp boat."

I jumped and turned to face him.

"Cindy, my wife, thought it would be a neat picture if we stood looking out through a shrimp net."

He handed me a glass of lemonade without even asking and I said thank you.

"It was taken when times were good," he said and took a swig of something more powerful than lemonade.

I looked around the living room. Every surface was covered with clothes or tools or papers. There was no indication that it was a room to live in. He watched me as I scanned the room but he didn't say anything.

"Where are your wife and daughter?"

"On the mainland. Cindy's working at a hotel and Stephanie is going to school there. We need dual incomes."

"Must be tough."

He laughed and took another swig. "Something tells me this isn't what you want to talk to me about."

"I overheard you and Wyatt talking."

I watched as the blood drained from his face. He remained silent.

"You paid him to give a fake vaccine to the horses."

He just stood there staring at me.

"Why would you do that?"

He didn't say anything for a very long time and I could see him struggling with himself.

"Revenge," he finally said.

"Revenge on whom?"

He took another swig and slammed the bottle down on the sideboard. "Stacey." The name came out covered in hatred. "She screwed up my life. I thought I could screw up hers a bit. Just a bit of a lark, you know? I just wanted to see her face when that first foal was born."

"So you thought she was for the vaccinations."

"What do you mean *thought*? I knew she was for them."

"Why would you think that?"

"Because she as much as told me."

"Did you know she was a devout Catholic?"

"What's that got to do with anything?"

"Maybe it would be hard for a Catholic to support birth control."

"Jesus, are you nuts? They're just horses," he said, but he looked unsure of himself.

"Maybe you just used the vaccine as a red herring. Or maybe she caught you paying Wyatt."

"What the hell are you talking about? I was just trying to screw up her life a bit, that's all."

"Maybe you permanently screwed up her life." That put me out his front door faster than I could have run.

I headed back to the research station on the trike. The sun was still low in the sky and lit up the branches of the live oaks with a golden wash. It was a weird sensation. I could feel the quiet of the forest even though I could not hear it above the noise of the trike. Endless pathways with no trace of civilization, other than the scuffmarks of the ATVs on the forest floor. Hard to believe that hundreds of cottages lay just out of sight. How could such an island have bred a killer? For all my rantings about the destructive attributes of ATVs I found myself loving the whip of the wind on my face and the sun cascading down through the trees. What is it about wind in our hair that makes us, as a species, want to fling up our arms in the air and yell for the sheer joy of it? I barrelled along the pathways, taking the puddles too fast and getting drenched for my troubles. I wheeled into the clearing like a pro and headed for my cabin and a clean set of clothes. Martha was sitting on her bed hunched over a computer as I breezed in.

"Cripes. What happened to you?"

I looked down at my mud-splattered clothes and resisted the urge to tell her three masked men had chased me clear across the island. When she heard my mundane explanation and looked disappointed I was rather sorry I hadn't lied. But she didn't let any moss grow on my words.

"I found something," she said. And then didn't say anything, just looked at me expectantly with a little twitchy smile on her face.

"On the computer?" I asked.

"On the computer and in the file."

"Okay. What is it?" I asked.

She remained annoyingly silent. If this was an *Aha* moment she was dragging it out for all it was worth.

Finally she said, "Okay. I was looking over Jayne's file and decided to surf the Nebraska State University website, hoping to find some mention of her. No luck. So I searched her name and, aside from all the papers she has written, and they are quite impressive, there was no personal information about her at all."

I started to take off my soaking pants and Martha continued, "So I phoned the university and pretended to be Jayne asking for a copy of her degree."

I was balanced on one leg when Martha let drop the next bit of information. "They had no record of any Gertrude Jayne ever attending Nebraska State University."

I sat down on my bed and stared at Martha. "But what about the degree?"

"It has to be a fake."

"But why would Jayne use a fake Ph.D.?"

"Because she never got a real one?"

chapter twenty

I finished getting into some dry clothes and was savagely scratching myself when Martha said, "Heads up." I turned in time to catch a tube of benzocaine.

"They say it helps with chiggers, that and washing all your clothes, cause they can hang around," she said.

I cracked open the tube and in my haste squirted some on my pants. "I hope they don't last as long as spider bites."

"Ten days and longer," said Martha.

I stared at her in horror. "What do you know about them? Oh, cripes. Do they burrow? Are they still all on me? Can they bite more than once?" I frantically frisked myself down.

"It's not the bite that itches, it's the saliva that they inject to liquefy your skin cells so they can eat."

"Charming," I said.

"It's actually pretty cool. You react to the saliva by hardening the cells along the saliva path and create a tube, just like a straw, with the chigger at one end drinking your skin cells. It's why it's so itchy.

"How do you know so much about chiggers?" I asked.

"Sam told me all about them when I asked why it wasn't a good idea to bushwhack."

"And when was that, pray tell?"

Martha looked at me and shrugged her shoulders. "Sorry, I forgot to tell you." She returned to the laptop and began tapping away.

I immediately collected my bushwhacking clothes, put them in a pillowslip, and threw them outside.

"Any other zingers besides the Ph.D.?"

She looked up at me and said, "There's a locked file labelled *Sinclair/Thompson*, but I can't get into it."

"Sinclair. Isn't that Wyatt's name?"

"Yeah, that's why I thought it might be interesting. The file is brand new. Only created five days ago but it's big, twenty megabytes."

"Photos?"

"Could be. Or scans of some kind. I went and looked at her download history and she downloaded a lot of stuff five days ago."

"Can't you access it that way? Through download history?"

"No. Something's blocking it."

"Okay. Then let's go for the password."

"Her name? Birth date? Barrier?"

"Turtles?"

Martha keyed in *Turtles* but nothing happened.

"Halifax? Dalhousie? McGill?"

We played around for a while but nothing worked and we finally gave up. But not before a new idea had hatched in my mind.

"How are you for running interference?" I asked.

"What have you got in mind?"

"I want to see if I can find the note Stacey wrote to Wyatt, the one that Wyatt mentioned the night Stacey announced the theft of the vaccine."

Martha's eyes widened. "You think he kept it?"

"Maybe not, but even if he threw it away garbage is picked up from the cabins only once a week so the chances are good that it is still around."

"How did you know that?" asked Martha.

I rustled around on the bedside table and found the letter to guests that had been left there for us to read. I gave it to Martha.

"Why do you want the note?"

"It might be the proof we need that Stacey was blackmailing Wyatt. It gives him a motive to kill her."

"How do you propose finding it?"

"I want to search his cabin over lunch. You could be my lookout."

Martha dumped the laptop on the bed beside her and said, "Ready when you are."

We planned it so that Martha would head up to lunch and once Wyatt was in the mess she would come out on the balcony to signal the all clear. I sat on the front porch of the cabin but the punkies and my own incessant itching chased me inside so I watched from behind the screen door. It seemed to take forever but finally Martha appeared and casually waved her hand. I hoped no one was watching her. Waving at nobody was very suspicious.

I made my move and walked quickly to Wyatt's cabin from mine by going behind the cabins so that I would be out of sight. Wyatt's cabin was almost the mirror image of my own. Two beds down each side separated by a table but with two cupboards along the wall at the foot of each bed. The room was a pigsty. Clothes and shoes flung everywhere and papers strewn all over the floor. His briefcase lay on the table on top of a pile of papers and the bed was almost completely unmade, with the fitted sheet halfway down the bed. I surveyed the papers on the floor — mostly blank sheets that must have fallen off the bed and then got underfoot. I searched through them all, and all the junk on both beds, but came up empty. I dumped the garbage can on the bed and started sorting through the contents. There were a lot of scrunched up papers — it appeared he was trying to write a research paper — but finally I found it. It was a little yellow paper and on it, handwritten, was:

Your vaccine is bogus. I'm willing to make a deal.
Stacey 25/9/86

Bull's eye. I stuffed it in my pocket and headed for the briefcase. I rifled through all the papers and was just about to give up when I spied a photo. It was a scan of a newspaper clipping. The girl in the photo was Melanie — or was it Stacey? In a scrum of media. As I lifted the photo out to take a better look a godawful ruckus erupted. Martha's voice pierced the air like a chainsaw. "Look everybody! Look! Look! It's a screech owl!" It hadn't exactly been the signal we had agreed upon but it worked wonders. I shoved the photo back into the briefcase, slammed the lid, and headed for the door. But I was too late. Martha hadn't given me enough time.

"Why are you following me?" The voice was high and angry but steady and very very close.

I practically dived under one of the beds and lay there in the thick dust with a pair of stinky boots for company, waiting.

"I need to hear it from you." Unmistakably Wyatt.

There was silence.

"I don't know what you are talking about and I don't want anything to do with you."

"You can't avoid it, Mel."

"Don't call me Mel. Only my friends call me that. Just leave me alone."

It was quiet for a long time after that and I was about to squirm out when I heard a footfall on the porch. The screen door opened. I could see his feet as he came in and sat down on the bed on top of me, making the mattress sag into my face. He sat there for a long time and it was all I could do not to sneeze or itch. He took my attention off my itchy legs when he picked up his cellphone and made a call.

"Arlene, baby, how are you?"

Silence.

"Yeah, yeah. I'm fine. The hurricane wasn't that bad."

Silence.

"Just a bad connection."

Silence.

"I need you to email me those results. Everything you've got on Melanie. Throw in what you have on Rosemary too."

Silence.

"No. No. I fired her."

Silence.

"Couldn't do her job."

Silence.

"Get right on it. I need it yesterday."

I heard the click of the cell shutting and then a huge sigh as he lifted his legs onto the bed. Five minutes later he was snoring away and I was stuck. I fervently hoped he wasn't one of those guys who took really long afternoon naps. At least a dozen itches were screaming for attention and it was agony not being able to scratch. Time went by as I mentally conquered one itch after the other that kept popping up. I was beginning to cramp up. I was eyeball to eyeball with one of his boots and I idly traced the pattern with my eyes for something to do. I stiffened. There in one of the grooves of the boot was a mangled cricket. I didn't have time to contemplate the significance of this because he let out a huge snort and sat up. I watched his feet move across the room and the sound of the screen door whining open was music to my ears. I waited a full minute before extricating myself from under the bed, frantically itching everywhere. The benzo whatever it was called had obviously worn off.

I crept to the door and looked out. Coast was clear and I hightailed it back to my cabin.

Martha was a mess.

"Oh, Cordi. I didn't know what to do. He just got up halfway through dinner and left. I couldn't think of anything else to do but cry screech owl."

"Did anyone leave before he did?"

She looked at me quizzically. "Yeah, Mel did. Why?"

I told her about the conversation I had overheard.

"You think Wyatt found out about Stacey and Melanie and was blackmailing them?"

"But why would their relationship be worth blackmail?"

"I don't know. But if they were about to expose him as a blackmailer, that gives Wyatt yet another motive for killing Stacey."

"Yeah, it does, doesn't it?"

"You found the note?"

"Yeah," I said and pulled the crumpled piece of paper out of my pocket.

Martha took it from me eagerly and smoothed it out on her bed. "Looks like blackmail to me," she said. "I wonder what sort of deal she had in mind. Money?"

"We may never know."

"He was in danger of being exposed in the vaccine debacle and he was blackmailing Stacey. Blackmailers blackmailing blackmailers."

"What are these numbers at the end of the note? 25/9/86," I asked.

"Obviously a date of some kind."

"But why a date twenty-four years ago?"

"Beats me. Maybe the year is just a mistake."

"I don't think so. It's too deliberate. It's got to have some other significance. We just have to find out what."

I slathered myself with more benzo while Martha puttered around the cabin, hooking up her printer to her computer again and loading paper, until I finally asked her what she was doing.

"All my night-vision photos. I want to print them out."

"You mean your new ones?"

"Yes."

So we shared our cabin amid the noise of an over-worked printer, with me on Stacey's laptop and Martha flitting back and forth between the printer, the computer, and her bed as it slowly filled with photos. The Internet was down so I looked into some of Stacey's files.

"Well I'll be dammed," I said after five minutes of nosing around.

Martha, who was peering at one of her photographs, looked up at me.

"Stacey was writing an autobiography."

"Lots of people do when they're given a death sentence."

"Yeah, but think what it means. If she was writing about something someone did not want disclosed …"

"It would give that someone a motive for murder." She dropped the photo she was holding onto the bed and said, "Did she use real names?"

I did a search for the first name that came to mind, *David*, and up he popped, multiple times.

"Try Melanie."

Nothing came up.

"The file was last dated more than three months ago, so I guess Melanie was not in the picture yet."

"If there's some bad stuff in there on David he might take offence."

I started searching through all the Davids, but my stomach was growling and I realized I had missed lunch. I set the computer aside, stood up, and stretched, the catlike kind of stretch that always feels so good.

"I'm going for some food." I said and opened the screen door to an onslaught of insects.

"This is getting all over the map, Cordi. We have too many motives to narrow things down."

"Or too many people," I said, as I walked out and let the door slam shut behind me.

I could hear Martha's voice trailing into the heat of afternoon as she asked me to get her a muffin and then it was quiet — the thick kind of quiet that blankets and smothers every cell in your mind, the complete absence of sound.

The mess was empty and I walked into the kitchen to check out the fridge. The only light was the one over the fridge and it gave off an eerie light that splayed shadows across the kitchen walls. I wondered when the shutters would come down.

I shuddered as I passed the door to the walk-in cooler, imagining Stacey in there all cold and lifeless.

In all that contemplation I didn't hear Darcy come in. He said "Hi," and his voice practically splattered me all over the ceiling.

"Sorry, didn't mean to scare you."

I tried to be nonchalant about it, but the fact was that anybody coming at me in the dark scared me.

"I just spoke to the police. It's still mayhem on the mainland and the living take precedence. It looks as though we were lucky here — we got the edge of the storm and the mainland got the brunt. A lot of buildings have been damaged and a lot of people killed. And they are short of staff. The long and the short of it is they couldn't give me a time when they would come. Between you and me I think they're being slow because we have decimated their crime scene."

"That's a harsh word."

"Well, it's true."

I had to admit he had a point. He reached out and opened the fridge and took out a pitcher of milk.

"A lot of people are complaining to me about your persistent questioning."

I didn't deign to answer. Instead I blocked him from closing the fridge, reached in, and pulled out a plateful of muffins and some apple juice.

"I found a copy of Stacey's will."

"Oh, Jesus — you never give up do you?"

"It says you get three percent."

"So?" No surprise there. And no comment about three percent being a piddly amount. He knew about the lottery and he knew about the will.

"So, three percent translates into more than a million dollars, but you knew that already, didn't you?" When he didn't answer me I said, "Did Stacey tell you?"

Instead of filling a glass with milk he put the pitcher down. "I am her clerk, her general dogs' body, her valet, her secretary. There is not much that she did that I didn't know about."

"Like the lottery?"

"Yeah. She won Lotto 649 when she was thirty-five and has been hounded ever since by speculators, charities, con artists."

"What about Melanie and Stacey?"

Darcy picked up the pitcher and poured himself some milk. "You know about that?"

"That Stacey is Melanie's mother? Yes."

For a moment I thought I saw a flash of something cross his face but whatever it was that was bothering him, he hid it well.

"Jayne told me that something happened to Stacey when she was younger that changed her outlook on life. Was that something Melanie?"

Darcy looked at me, mouth open, and I could tell he was searching for the right words. "Yeah, you could sort of say that." He had a habit of using that phrase.

When I pressed him for more information he clammed up.

"What about the crickets?" I said into the growing silence.

"Crickets?"

"Stacey's snake. Did she always keep it in her cabin?"

He looked at me curiously. "No, it was always at her cottage."

"Except the day she died."

"Yeah. She brought it from the cottage because of the hurricane."

"And the crickets? Where did they come from?"

"A wholesaler on the mainland. I brought her the box the evening she died. We keep them in the walk-in fridge."

"And she spilled them." It seemed sort of sad somehow that one of the last things Stacey did was chase after some liberated crickets whose chirping was driving her crazy.

"Yeah, but she must have got them all because I don't remember seeing or hearing any when we found her body."

"Not all of them," I said under my breath. "Not all of them."

chapter twenty-one

I left Darcy and sat down at one of the lines of tables in the mess. The rows reminded me, with a shudder, of *Madeline*, the little kid's story about an orphanage that had so disturbed me as a child; all those neat little rows of perfectly made beds, so devoid of humanity. I shoved *Madeline* out of my mind and found an old copy of *International Wildlife*. I was reading it while eating my second muffin when I heard someone coming down the hall toward me. I looked up and squinted but they were backlit and I couldn't see who it was. I coughed to let them know I was there, my meeting with Darcy still forefront in my mind.

Despite my warning whoever it was gave a little squeal, just like a mouse, and then said, "Is that you, Cordi?"

"Just having a snack," I said. "I missed lunch."

"Yeah, we noticed." Rosemary. "Where were you?"

I made a mental note to try and teach myself not to volunteer information when it wasn't asked for.

"Just lost track of time on the beach," I ad libbed.

She went into the kitchen and rummaged around before she came over and joined me, carrying a plateful of cookies and a Diet Pepsi. The two seemed incongruous together somehow, but I suppose she could have been one of those people who like the taste of Diet Pepsi. She certainly didn't need the diet part of it. Or maybe she was diabetic? In the dim light of the mess I could hardly make out the injuries to her face and I caught myself staring. So did she.

She gave me a tentative smile. "The swelling's gone down," she said.

"Or maybe it was never there?"

She almost choked on her cookie as she turned to stare at me. "Why would you ever say that?"

"I overheard you and Wyatt talking. He as much as accused you of telling people he beats you."

"So?"

"So are the bruises makeup?"

She stared at the cookies on her plate and I watched her swallow hard several times.

"Do you know anything about men who beat women?" Her voice was low and even. "Sometimes you have to placate them to avoid another beating. That's all it was. Survival. I was just telling him what he wanted to hear. He's a dangerous man and I wouldn't put it past him if he killed Stacey."

"Why do you say that?"

"He's got a dark past."

"What sort of dark past?"

She hesitated and I got the feeling she wasn't sure she should say anymore. But she did. "Just search

Wyatt Thompson on the Internet and don't ever tell him I said that."

"But his last name's Sinclair."

"One of his many last names is Sinclair."

I asked her all the questions you could imagine I would want to ask her after that retort but she politely dodged them all. I made a mental note to surf the web as soon as it was back online.

We were sitting side by side, munching cookies and muffins, when she jumped up with a squeal and said, "I forgot to put the ice cream back." When I looked confused she said, "I was going to have ice cream but decided not to."

I watched her walking to the kitchen and wondered at how vulnerable she seemed. Could she have faked a beating? And if so, why would she do that? The only possible motive would be to make Wyatt look bad. Again, why would she want to do that? There was another little squeal from the kitchen and the sound of something falling. I got up and walked to the doorway. She was standing over a tub of ice cream that had fallen on the floor. The door to the walk-in cooler was open.

"I forgot," she moaned.

I reached past her and shut the door, suppressing my own little shiver as I did so.

She looked at me and shook her head "I know I wasn't there or anything but I can't get an image of her out of my head with her hands tied with slip knots and her legs tied to the chair too. And now this," and she nodded her head in the direction of the walk-in fridge.

"Did you know her well?" I asked, wondering why I suddenly felt ill at ease.

"She was my friend," said Rosemary.

"Where did you meet her?"

Rosemary looked momentarily confused. "She was at a vet conference and we shared a room." When I looked puzzled she said, "When attendees don't have enough money they have subsidized rooms, but you've got to share."

But that was not what I was looking puzzled about. "What was she doing at a vet conference?"

"She was scouting around getting information on vaccinating horses."

"Is that how the islanders got Wyatt? Through you and Stacey?"

She hesitated and stooped to pick up the ice cream. As she did so I caught a look of total panic on her face. She stood up, clutching the ice cream in her hands. But she didn't meet my eye; instead she looked in the direction of the fridge and shuddered. "Gives me the creeps," she said, as if no question lay unanswered between us. She went and replaced the ice cream in the right fridge and then left me alone to contemplate the contents of the wrong fridge and the rows of empty tables behind me. In the winter the tables would have been insufferably depressing to me but it was summer and my mind was clear and free of the darkness that always stalked it in the wintertime.

I left the mess and moved out onto the verandah. I moved to the edge to take in the view and as I leaned on the wraparound railing I felt it give. I kicked out and jumped back, then moved forward again to cautiously look over the edge. It was a twenty-foot drop with death waiting at the bottom. My heart was beating like a jackhammer as

I went back inside to look for some orange tape to flag it. As I headed for the store room I passed Jayne, sitting in a lab festooned with turtles — posters, coasters, sculptures, and paintings. They were everywhere.

"Cordi!" She called out. "I wanted to talk to you."

I restrained myself from saying I wanted to talk to her too.

"One of the turtle nests is due up tonight. I thought you and Martha might like to go and wait for it to come up. No guarantees, of course, but I know Martha really wants to get pictures of a nest erupting."

Erupting? That word seemed a bit extreme. I mean, how fast can turtles be?

"It should happen anytime before dawn."

"Is it only ever at night?"

"Yup. It's the drop in temperature at night that activates them." She paused and said, "Look, if a nest comes up — its number forty-two, on the stick in the middle, you'll see — would you mind counting them and then releasing them to the sea?"

I nodded and then asked her if she had any orange tape, but before she could answer I rushed in, "Stacey knew about you, didn't she?"

She stiffened at that and looked up at me. I took a reasoned guess. "You never got a Ph.D., did you?"

She looked away and I thought she wasn't going to answer me, but she did. "No," she said, and I wondered how long she had sat on her secret.

"How did Stacey find out?"

"She wanted my job so she went searching for something to hold over me."

"And she found it."

"Yeah. She told me if I didn't resign as director she'd tell the Island Association."

"That must have made you very angry. To have that hanging over your head. To lose your job," I said.

"What do you think? Of course it did."

"Enough to kill her?"

She looked at me and sighed. "How very dramatic, Cordi, but you're barking up the wrong tree."

"Am I?" I said, but I was unsure of myself because she was so sure of herself.

"It's just a Ph.D. It's not the end of my life."

"But it would be the end of your career, and I know how much you love your job."

She looked at me then and didn't answer. Instead she opened a drawer and handed me a roll of scotch tape. "Bring it back when you're done." She made a point of going back to her work.

I looked at the tape — fat lot of good it would do — and put it back on her desk mumbling something about how it wouldn't work.

I was beginning to feel like a pariah — alienating everyone. It is such a negative thing, investigating a murder when everybody is a suspect.

There was only one killer so the other seven had a right to be angry with me.

I spent the rest of the afternoon walking the beach, reading, and then taping birds. I must have been very tired because I fell asleep to the sounds of the surf pounding on the beach. When I woke up it was getting dark and the benzo had worn off. I was still thinking about Jayne as I made my way back to my cabin, itching and scratching so much that I must have looked like a marionette.

Martha was snoring on the bed but woke up when the screen door banged shut.

"Wake up. We're going on the hunt."

She sat up so quickly I thought she might have given herself whiplash. "Who's the suspect?" she asked eagerly.

"Not that kind of hunt. We're after turtle hatchlings." And I told her what Jayne had told me.

Martha spent the next fifteen minutes getting all her camera gear and binoculars ready. When I pointed out that we would be inches away from the nest she brushed it off by saying you never knew what might walk into your lens. She quickly showed me how to use the still camera so that she could film it with the night-vision scope. Then we both spent a lot of time dressing in long-sleeved shirts and long pants and tucking our pant legs into our socks. I wore a T-shirt underneath my long-sleeved shirt so that the punkies, if they broke through my first line of defence, would hit the T-shirt and be stymied. And I had slathered myself with benzo. When we were done, all that was exposed were our faces and Martha threw me a bottle of something called Skin so Soft to smear on my face — a perfume invented for attraction had become the arsenal for fending off biting insects. I remembered Sam on that first night and how I had thought he must have been a bit effeminate to be wearing it despite his enormous size. But ya do what ya gotta do to stymie the little devils.

It was very dark when we mounted the trike and took off through the woods. I had been to the hatchery once before but I lost my way twice. If it hadn't been for the moon I would have missed the turnoff to Hunter's house. I led Martha down the narrow footpath to the clearing and heard her catch her breath. It was a full moon and the house stood in stark black relief against the white sands of the dunes.

The charred windows, like unseeing eyes, and the open mouth of the door made it look like a dark cartoon of a house, old and broken down and unwanted. It was eerie and creepy in its decay.

Martha didn't say a word as we made our way past the house and down into the dunes. And there it was — the hatchery, a twenty-by-twenty-foot enclosure nestled among the dunes on a flat section of the upper beach. Sturdy fencing enclosed it and inside were twelve circular fences that were about six inches tall with a diameter of about eighteen inches, each representing a nest. I went over to the main fence, put a hand on the metal post, and nearly screamed. The electric fence zapped me — the surprise was probably worse than the bite, but I couldn't help wonder why Jayne hadn't told me. Martha and I found the box with the switch, which fortunately wasn't locked, and turned it off.

"Why the hell would they electrify the fence?" asked Martha.

"Probably to keep the predators out," I said. "The feral pigs love to dig up these nests and feast on the eggs. So do the coons and the ghost crabs and the seagulls, once the young have hatched, and then all kinds of predators in the sea. They say only about one percent of sea turtle hatchlings ever make it to maturity."

"Poor little guys."

"Did you know there are only six species of sea turtle? These guys are loggerheads. Caretta caretta."

"How did you know that?"

"I did a paper once in high school."

We climbed the fence and found the marker for nest forty-two, a numbered stick planted right in the middle of the circular fencing. Martha wanted to remove the stick for better pictures but I said we'd better wait until we saw some action in case the nest didn't come up and we had to put the stick back in and maybe do some damage. I sat down on the sand and eyeballed the nest while Martha got out her equipment. And then we just sat and talked and stared at that nest as clouds slowly obliterated the moon. We could hear thunder in the distance somewhere. I brought Martha up-to-date on all my discoveries.

"I'm beginning to think more and more that Wyatt killed Stacey."

"Because she was blackmailing him?" said Martha.

"That and the crickets."

"Crickets?"

"There was a squashed cricket in the sole of his boot and Stacey was the only one at the station who used crickets as food for her pet snake."

"And?"

"So the timeline, according to Darcy, has Stacey spilling her crickets all over her cabin just before 11:30 and killing them off," I said. "Meaning Wyatt was in her cabin sometime after 11:30."

"But maybe it was a native cricket that he stepped on," said Martha.

"Could be, but how easy is it to step on a live cricket in the woods. They are pretty fast, you know."

"But he could have stepped on a dead one that Stacey left lying about. That's more likely." She had a point.

"So he lied about his whereabouts?" asked Martha.

"Wouldn't you lie too? I mean, it puts him at the scene of the crime and with an okay motive. And why did he want Mel's file?" I filled Martha in.

"Maybe he knows they were mother and daughter?" said Martha.

"But why would that change anything?"

"Maybe he thought Stacey had confided in her daughter and that she would just continue the blackmail," I said.

"Sounds farfetched to me. Anyway, why would he want Rosemary's file too?"

"No way of knowing if we don't know what's in them."

We sat in silence as the storm gathered around us, and I thought about the little sea turtles lying somewhere beneath the sand. Hopefully they had already hatched out in their nest some eighteen inches beneath the surface, breaking the leathery egg with the little white pipping tooth on their snouts. If they were already out of their eggs the top layer of turtles would be scratching at the sand on the ceiling of the oval-shaped womb and the bottom layer would be trampling the loose sand as it sifted down from above. In this way the whole chamber would slowly rise to the surface where we were waiting.

I think I dozed off for a second after that because next thing I knew Martha was yelling, "They're coming, they're coming," and I had to shake my head to remember who was coming and that it wasn't some sort of attacking force. I grabbed Martha's camera and peered over at the nest as she removed the stick. There was a telltale dimpling of the sand and then, miraculously, the shape of a single tiny sand-covered head emerged. And then the nest erupted. With flippers flying and bodies squirming, the sand turned into a boiling mass of churning bodies, dozens upon dozens of them. Three hours of no-see-ums and mosquitoes and it was all over in less than a minute; more than a hundred little baby sea turtles thrashing around inside their little enclosure, frantically searching for the sea.

Martha and I carefully counted the turtles into a bucket and then we walked out through the dunes and down to the sea. I slowly tipped the bucket over and watched as one hundred and two sea turtles tumbled out. Several fell on their backs and squirmed and twisted to right themselves. The vanguard made a beeline down the beach to the waves and the wild seas beyond. They were so strong and vigorous — the instinct to head to the sea overpowering all else. No wonder Jayne was such a turtle supporter. Just watching these little guys as they were washed back up the beach by waves many times stronger than they were gave real meaning to the word *persistent*.

And then, out of nowhere, the skies erupted and the rain came down in torrents. We could see lighting strike down the beach and that had us heading back up into the dunes faster than the sea turtles. It was a wild, wicked storm and even though we both knew not to hide in the forest the open dunes seemed worse. We plummeted down a dune into the cover of the trees. I had my flashlight on and once we got down to the forest floor I turned it off for a second. I had the totally irrational thought that maybe with the flashlight off the lightning couldn't see us. It somehow didn't seem fair to get such a storm on the heels of a hurricane.

We were soaking wet and enormously tired by the time we finally found our way back to the trike and then back home to the station and our snug little cabin.

"Cordi, this has got to stop. All these attempts on your life," said Martha out of the blue.

"Oh c'mon, Martha. You can't really call a bad storm an attempt on my life."

"I don't mean the storm," she said in exasperation. "Don't you see? Someone is trying to scare you, not kill you. At least, I think that's what it means, because they could have killed you if they really wanted to. But why?"

"Maybe they've destroyed evidence I saw that the police would never know about if I got scared off."

And that's when it hit me. What had been missing when we carried Stacey's body up to the fridge: the ropes on her hands were gone.

It was 3:00 in the morning when my head finally hit the pillow and even Martha's snoring didn't wake me up. I woke the next morning and lay in bed, my thoughts storming through my mind like last night's lightning.

Into this maelstrom came two words spoken loudly, "Holy shit."

Always nice to wake to that, I thought and rolled over on my elbow to find Martha sitting on her made bed, Stacey's laptop open in front of her. She raised her eyes at me and said, "Bingo." Silently, she handed me the laptop as I sat up.

I took it on my lap and pushed the screen back so I could see.

"MAN ARRESTED ON RAPE CHARGES" was the headline. It was a picture of a man trying to shield his face from the cameras and surrounded by police. I looked up at Martha, puzzled.

"Look at his face," she said. I saw it then, his face a lot younger and a little slimmer and his hair dark brown, but it was unmistakably Wyatt.

"Look at the date of the rape," said Martha.

September 25, 1986.

chapter twenty-two

"Where did you find this stuff?" I asked Martha as I scrolled through the news item.

"It was in the locked file called *Sinclair/Thompson*," she said. The same name Rosemary had told me to search.

"But the password?"

"I remembered what you said about Stacey loving sea turtles. And I remembered you called the hatchlings last night *Caretta caretta*."

"The Latin name for the loggerhead sea turtle," I said.

"So I tried Caretta2."

"September 25, 1986." I scanned through the article and there it was: Stacey — she'd been eighteen at the time and home alone. It didn't say much more than that and so we flipped through some of the other clippings, some of which dealt with a different case, to glean more information. I keyed in the name and more articles popped up. But there was very little detail on exactly what had happened. Then Martha had the brilliant idea of looking through Stacey's autobiography. Half an hour later I had found the entry. I read it out loud to Martha.

It was the trees that really bothered me. Their dark shadows spilled across the sidewalk and the branches blocked the streetlights. When I looked up, their shiny green leaves were dull, black and menacing. I began to walk faster — I was only a block away. A pebble scraped on the sidewalk and I whirled. I couldn't be sure, but I thought I saw a dark silhouette among the shadows of the trees. Just my imagination. I stepped off the curb onto the narrow suburban road where the streetlights lit me up and made me feel both vulnerable and safe. I tried to block out the images coalescing inside my brain like so many unwanted wasps. I started to run. Only a block away. As I stopped and listened I heard the braking footfall of someone behind me. I turned to look, scanning the sidewalk, but it was too dark to see. Was I hearing things? I began walking again, resisting the urge to flee hysterically into the night.

My house was just past the Wilsons' who were long since in bed. As my house came into view I stopped, momentarily confused. There were no lights on. None. The house stood dark, silent, and soulless. I shivered and looked behind me. No one. I approached the front door. Why had my parents not left the lights on? They had said they would. Promised they would. There was no car in the driveway either. Where were they? Had they forgotten I was coming home tonight? One year away at college and they'd forgotten me?

I grabbed the knob on the front door and turned. It was locked. Thank god it was locked. The Wilsons' dog began barking and I quickly inserted my key in the lock and let myself in. I'd never come home to an empty house before. It seemed so alien, so cold. Where was Chili? He should have been at the front door to greet me. I turned on the switch and flooded the hall and the front stairs with light. A note on the bottom stair. I picked it up.

Grama had a heart attack. They'd call. I held back a sob, scrunched the note up. Had my parents taken the dog with them? To the hospital?

Cautiously I entered the living room, groping for the switch on the wall. From dark indefinable shapes the living room leapt to life with the familiar black leather sofa and matching chair, the Blackwood print over the fireplace, my mother's silver candelabra with five red candles — always red — wall-to-wall bookcases, and the double window and back door to the yard, leading off the living room. It took me awhile to notice it, because it was very subtle, but the sheer curtain covering the eight little windows on the backdoor was moving. My heart rate went up as I stared, willing it to stop its gentle billowing. Gingerly I approached and pulled back the curtain. My heart stopped for a blinding instant. Someone had broken the window closest to the lock. Someone was in the house.

I whirled around, looking for a weapon, saw the candelabra and grabbed it. I had to get out of the house. I was moving silently through the living room back toward the front door, when a movement on the stairs to the second floor made me look up into a face of terror. A large man with a nylon stocking deforming his face, making it grotesque, stood at the top of the stairs, his right hand holding a baseball bat.

I fled to the phone in the kitchen, putting the candelabra on the counter, but it fell on the floor — the loud clanging noise a hideous beacon of where I was. I tried to dial 911 while the panic clawed its way into my mind, enveloping it and infecting it with its contagion. The sight of one dangling wire drilled its way into my brain and I dropped the phone, picked up the candelabra, and ran for the back door where I nearly tripped over him — Chili, lying on his side right in front of the door, as if guarding it for me. Too late. I could see that from the way his little neck lay at an unnatural angle, that and the sightless eyes. I felt nauseated as I frantically moved Chili out of the way with my foot and unlocked the door. I only got it partway open when out of the corner of my eye I saw the baseball bat arcing down toward my head with vicious speed. I threw up the candelabra in defence and I tried to duck, but the blow was shattering and the darkness complete.

I stopped reading. "That's it. Christ. He must have raped her when she was unconscious," I said. "She just talks about the horrors of the rape kit and how that made her feel. Nothing about the rape."

"Why did he get off?" asked Martha.

I skimmed through the pages.

"Oh boy. Her brother bribed a judge and the case was sent to retrial but was thrown out on a technicality. Actually, key evidence, including the rape kit, went missing after the bribe was discovered." I looked up. "David bribed a judge."

"That doesn't sound good."

"It says here that he hoped the judge would convict Wyatt. Instead it led to Wyatt's release."

"No wonder he and Stacey didn't get along very well. David tries to help her and ends up ruining her chances of seeing her rapist go to jail," said Martha.

"If this book is published he can kiss his job as a lawyer goodbye."

"If he knows about the book. Gives him another dynamite motive."

"What about Wyatt? He comes to Spaniel Island and Stacey recognizes him. She must be really bitter that he walked free and suddenly she has two things to hold over him, the fake vaccine and the rape. He's turned himself into a respectable guy with a new name. He's not going to want her ruining that. So he kills her."

"It all fits. He beats women. At least, we think he does. He rapes Stacey. He fakes the vaccine. He kills Stacey," said Martha.

"Yeah, but too many other people have motives almost as good."

"But we can't place them at the scene of the crime."

"You mean the cricket?"

Martha looked at me as if she knew I was about to do something stupid, which I was. "What are you thinking, Cordi?"

"That I need to have a talk with Wyatt."

"Not alone you're not."

Duncan waylaid Martha in our search for Wyatt – so much for her worries. I bumped into David in my meanderings and pigeonholed him.

"It seems you have another motive," I said as he made an effort to detach himself from me.

He puffed out his cheeks. "Do you ever let up?"

"She was writing an autobiography."

He looked startled for a moment and then regained his composure.

"So you knew?" I asked.

"Yes, of course I knew. She did talk to me, you know, from time to time."

"So you know she detailed your bribe to the judge all those years ago. Before you were even a lawyer, no doubt."

"Yes, I knew."

"Was she aware of what it could do to your career if it got out?"

"I tried to reason with her but it didn't work. She always blamed me for the fact that her rapist went free."

"So you killed her."

"Oh, for God's sake. I didn't kill her."

"So who did?" I said.

"You tell me," he retorted.

"Maybe nobody," I said and then wondered why I'd said it.

He looked at me strangely and was about to say something, when Darcy happened upon us. He looked from me to David and said, "Interrupting something?"

To which David replied, "Not at all," and he turned hastily and left.

I asked Darcy where Wyatt was. He said Wyatt had gone to the local watering hole, which had reopened, and he gave me directions.

"Are the boats running again?"

"Yup. They started first thing this morning and there are a gazillion islanders coming over to look at the damage."

"What about the police?"

"They said they are coming, maybe later this afternoon or evening."

I waved to Darcy and headed toward the watering hole.

I was feeling pretty good. What safer place than a restaurant to confront Wyatt? Delsey's Spot was an A-frame building on stilts with a huge balcony full of tables, most of which were empty. I scanned them all but Wyatt wasn't there.

I went inside, where it took a moment for my eyes to adjust. The restaurant was one big marine motif. There was a bar built like a small jetty with bar stools made out of the spoked wooden steering wheels of boats — nicely capped with thick Plexiglas, for the sake of comfort. Various fishing nets festooned the walls, punctuated by buoys of all sizes and colours.

Wyatt was sitting at a booth right by the tall plate-glass windows that overlooked the balcony. One thing was consistent about this island: no one had a view of the sea from any building. It made the beach feel isolated and free, but it made the buildings feel claustrophobic and lacking in something. But they made up for whatever it was by being built on stilts with wonderful staircases and wraparound verandahs.

I called him by name and he looked up in surprise.

"May I join you?"

"Do I have a choice?"

I took that as a yes and slid in along the vinyl-upholstered bench.

He'd been reading a paper and nursing a coffee. He made a point of carefully folding the paper and placing it on the table.

"I know all about you," I said.

"No you don't," he said, matter-of-factly.

Not a good start. I didn't like being on the defensive.

"I've read the articles about September 25, 1986," I said.

"I was acquitted." He pinioned my eyes with his steely gaze. I couldn't get over how calm he was. It was unnatural.

"On a technicality," I said.

"What's your point?" he asked irritably.

"That as far as Stacey was concerned you are as guilty as they come."

"Too bad she's dead."

"Too bad you killed her."

He laughed at that and said, "Too bad you have no proof." He was enjoying this so I went for the jugular.

"I found a cricket in your boot."

He looked at me quizzically. "How would you know what was on my boot?" he asked and I kicked myself for not preparing an answer to that. So I ignored him.

"It puts you at the scene of the crime." And I told him about the spilled crickets.

"Conviction by cricket? Can't you do better than that?"

"It means you lied. You were in Stacey's cabin that night."

"Precisely — that night — it only means I was there sometime after the crickets escaped, but it is all speculation anyway. It wasn't me."

"How can you say that?"

"My boots were taken from my cabin the afternoon that Stacey was killed and someone returned them the following morning."

I tried to hide my surprise. I had not thought of that scenario.

"Are you a diabetic?" I asked.

"What has that got to do with anything?"

"So you are?"

He moved his hand up to his neck as if looking for something and then let it drop. He gave an imperceptible nod.

I said, "Your MedicAlert necklace was found in Stacey's hand."

"So that's where it went," he said.

"So you admit to struggling with Stacey, who ripped off your necklace while you were killing her."

"This is getting tedious. I did not kill Stacey."

"So how do you explain your necklace in her hand?"

"It was taken the same afternoon."

"Someone just strolled up to you and took it from around your neck?" I said.

"Oh, for Christ's sake. No. I took it off to take a sauna and it was gone when I got back."

"Why didn't you tell someone?"

"Why would I want everyone to know I'm a diabetic?"

I changed tacks. "What did Stacey tell you when you met?"

"I didn't recognize her. She was big and fat, not at all like the lithe little thing who cried rape."

The waitress came and interrupted us. I ordered a tea as he said, "Don't make yourself too comfortable here. I'm only humouring you, you know. It's really rather stimulating to think you think I'm a murderer," he said, his eyes sharp and piercing.

I tried again. "What did you talk about?"

"Our twenty-five year reunion? What does anyone talk about? Husbands, wives, kids, dogs, cats."

I sat there stone-faced and he said, "Oh, lighten up, Cordi. It's not all bad." But I didn't lighten up. "Okay. Okay. She told me she'd drag everything up again and see I was devetted, if there is such a word."

"What did she want in return?"

He laughed.

"It couldn't have been money."

"No, it couldn't. She was one fat wealthy bitch, wasn't she?" he said as he took another sip of what had to be stone-cold coffee.

The waitress arrived with my tea and I waited for him to continue.

"No," he said, "it wasn't money. She wanted me to promise to keep a secret." He started laughing.

"What secret?"

"Never to tell Mel that I was her father."

He looked at me and laughed again. "You didn't know?" I felt sick.

"But that means she had proof that you raped her. Your own daughter. Her DNA. Your DNA."

"Oh come on. Be real. It was consensual."

"A baseball bat over the head is consensual?"

"You're assuming I am guilty but there's no reason to believe the rapist is Melanie's father. Stacey obviously had intercourse with more than one man."

He was daring me to agree with him and I was feeling slightly unwell.

"Besides, if it was me, which it wasn't, I'd have to say Stacey played the martyr card. She would rather save her daughter from ever knowing me than see me in jail. How's that for female idiocy?"

I tried to ignore him but he was getting to me. "But if you are the rapist you'd damn well have to get rid of Stacey."

"Back to that again, are we? You're pathetic. So was she." He laughed again. "It was so deliciously funny." He fixed me with his glacial eyes. "Aren't you going to ask me why?"

"Why?"

"Because until she told me I had no idea Mel was my daughter." He laughed again. "Stupid bitch."

chapter twenty-three

After Wyatt left I sat at the table and counted the number of starfish in the fishing nets on the wall. My form of meditation, I guess. I had reached number thirty-seven when a bell tinkled and I looked up to see Sam coming through the front door. He didn't see me sitting there and went over to the woman behind the bar.

"Hey, Linda Lee. Can you give me a whirly burger and fries to go?"

"Ten minutes, Sam."

"No problem." He was perched halfway onto a bar stool and he turned to survey the room and caught my eye, which wasn't hard since it was on him the whole way and I was the only person in the place. He slid off the bar stool and headed my way.

"Cordi, what are you doing in here?" he asked.

"Same as you."

"No, I mean, why are you inside? It's a beautiful day out there."

I looked outside and said, "Have a seat."

He looked around as if trying to find a way out but there was none so he sat down facing me.

I cut to the chase. "Why are you ignoring Mel?"

He looked at me in surprise. "You're pretty blunt."

I sat in silence, waiting. People abhor silence and if you can outlast the other guy it usually pays off. It didn't this time.

"What's come between you and Mel? You told me the other day that she wasn't who she seemed. What did you mean by that?"

Sam fiddled with a knife on the table spinning it around and around, until I reached out and stopped it.

"When Wyatt came she changed. She used to be so outgoing and happy. And now she's all closed up and brittle. Not the woman I signed on for," he said bitterly.

"There's more, isn't there?"

"Why do you say that?" he warily asked.

"Because you don't ditch someone after only five days of unexplained bad vibes. Not when you've been with her all summer. If you love them you hang in there."

He reached for the knife again and I let him take it.

"When I said she'd changed she said it was because she wasn't who she thought she was and that I should just get used to it or get lost. I got lost."

"But you didn't want to get lost, did you?"

"No, I didn't," he spat angrily. "But she scared me." He glared at me.

"Why does she scare you, Sam?" I asked quietly.

"Because I think maybe she murdered Stacey."

"Why would you think that?" I watched him fiddling with the knife and wrestling with his demons.

"Because she told me she was Stacey's daughter." He glanced up quickly, waiting for my reaction, and immediately looked down again. "And Stacey was leaving her twenty million dollars. I knew Mel had a shitty upbringing. Who wouldn't blame their mother for that?"

"I can see why you might think what you did. It's a good motive."

"Do you think she did it?" Sam's hand froze in midair and he looked up at me with eyes so intense they could have cut like diamonds.

"There are others with equally good motives," I said, almost like a refrain.

Sam slammed his hand down on the table. "That's just it. My head says she could be a murderer and my heart says no. If I really love her I shouldn't doubt her. Love doesn't seem to be blind for me, which must mean I don't love her." He looked up with such torment on his face that I didn't know how to answer. Luckily I was rescued by Linda Lee and the whirly burger, whatever that was.

Sam took his burger outside without saying goodbye and I decided to order a whirly burger. While I waited for it to come I entertained myself by trying to find my location on the tabletop nautical charts that lay under a thick sheet of acrylic. The burger was taller than my mouth and came by its name honestly. It was so hot it made my head whirl and I had to order two drinks to put out the fire. I paid my bill and walked out onto the verandah. Sam was right. It was much nicer outside.

As I was heading for the stairs someone called out my name. I turned and saw Martha waving at me, so I went over and said hello. She and Melanie were sitting at a table together. I looked around for Sam but he seemed to have made himself scarce. I sat down beside Martha and opposite Melanie, feeling butterflies in my stomach. I really didn't want to talk to Mel.

"How's the sleuthing going?" said Martha.

"It's a mess. Everybody still has a motive." I looked at Mel but she was taking in the view. "Including you, Mel." She froze and slowly swivelled to look at me.

"Meaning what?"

"Twenty million dollars is a lot of money."

She looked trapped.

"We know that Stacey was your mother."

"So?" she said defiantly.

"So she was a very wealthy woman."

"And you think I'd kill her for her money? I finally find my mother after all these years and you have me killing her?" She was half standing now and I waited until she caught her breath and sat down.

"You told me you hated your mother, that she abandoned you. Why the sudden reversal?" She stared at me but remained quiet, her face a tableau of confusion and anger.

"Would your father have wanted her dead?"

She stared at me unblinking, her face frozen, her eyes bulging, and in that instant I knew she knew.

"My father?"

"Wyatt." She did a pretty good job of choking on her own saliva and Martha was all over her while darting the evil eye at me. But when Mel finally raised her eyes they were clear and steady. Without speaking she gathered her things and left. I was spared a tongue lashing from Martha when Duncan appeared at our table and took a seat. The waitress came and took their orders, and even though I warned against the whirly burger Duncan threw caution to the wind.

"Apparently the ferry is up and running so you ladies will be able to leave tomorrow morning as planned," said Duncan.

Martha and I looked at each other and grimaced.

"What? You don't want to leave?" asked Duncan.

"No, no it's just that this case is getting to us ... me." I realized Martha's grimace had been for something entirely different as she gazed fondly at Duncan.

I filled Duncan and Martha in on all that had transpired. Martha was fidgeting like a woman with ants in her pants, or like me itching my legs.

When I finally finished she said, "I've got another piece of the puzzle." She looked around at us triumphantly. "I searched the name that Rosemary gave to you, Wyatt Thompson, on the Internet. There were multiple references to a second trial."

We looked at her expectantly.

"They had to do with the murder of a young woman in Austin, Texas."

She waited for us to say something so I humoured her. "What has that got to do with anything?"

"The young woman was Jennifer Nesbitt and her killer was acquitted for lack of evidence."

When Duncan and I looked bewildered she said, "Jennifer Nesbitt was Rosemary Nesbitt's sister."

I let that bit of information percolate and then said, "And the killer?" But I already knew.

"Wyatt Thompson."

After that little bombshell we sat in silence for a while. I ordered another drink from the waitress. Duncan ordered two more and quaffed them both almost in one go as soon as they arrived. I was very proud of myself — I didn't say a thing.

"Isn't Rosemary Wyatt's assistant?" asked Duncan.

"Interesting, eh?" I said. "I mean, why would the sister of the woman Wyatt allegedly killed take on a job working for her sister's murderer?"

"And what does that have to do with Stacey's murder?"

"If anybody, Rosemary would want Wyatt dead."

"Rosemary, Mel, Sam, Trevor, David, Jayne, even Darcy all have solid motives," said Martha.

"But Wyatt is our best bet," and I told Duncan about the MedicAlert and the cricket.

"So we can put him at the scene of the crime?" said Duncan. I nodded but suddenly remembered Wyatt and how he had refuted everything I said and how I had felt unwell. I felt unwell again. Was I beginning to believe Wyatt?

Martha jerked me out of my thoughts by saying, "How could Stacey have made so many enemies?"

"She didn't," Duncan said. "Only one of these people killed her, the rest are motives only. They only become real if you're the murderer."

I thought back to the murder scene. Something in

my subconscious was waving frantically and my conscious mind was trying valiantly to catch up. Something to do with the murder scene. I pictured it again in my mind. Stacey tied with those horrid slip knots to the chair, the necklace clenched in her fist, the smell of chloroform, the medical texts. And, like a face emerging from the depths of a lake, there it was in my mind, where it had been all along.

"Stacey was tied to the chair with slip knots."

Martha and Duncan looked at me with interest.

"You never told us they were slip knots," Duncan said.

"Who uses slip knots to tie a person up?" I asked.

"Most people would use a reef knot or some other knot that's easier to tie," said Martha.

"And more effective at binding the hands," said Duncan.

"So why use a slip knot?" But I already knew. I just had to check the crime scene again and then I'd be sure.

chapter twenty-four

I told Duncan and Martha to meet me at the scene of the crime — I'd always wanted to say that — and I took the quickest route back to the station, where I picked up a bunch of supplies, and then headed over to Stacey's. I was peering through Stacey's door when I heard Martha and Duncan arriving. I had each of them look inside at the chair and the desk.

"The layout is similar to ours, except Stacey just had one bed," I said to Martha.

"What are you getting at, Cordi?" asked Duncan.

"I want to recreate something for you, but we obviously can't do it here."

I led them back along the path to my cabin and had them both sit on one of the beds. I pulled out the chair and sat down in it. I tied one of my ankles to each leg the way Stacey had been tied. Then I tied four pillows around my chest and stomach to simulate Stacey. I took the cloth, dunked it in pretend chloroform, pressed it quickly to my face, and then threw it away. I picked up the duct tape, took a section and ripped it from the roll, then lay it on my lap. I took another section of duct tape and put it over my mouth. Using a slip knot, I tied one hand to the chair. On the other I prefashioned a slip knot, tying the loose end to the chair and leaving a large noose at the other, and left it on my right leg. Duncan caught his breath but I continued. I placed the duct tape over my nose and then slipped my free hand through the noose and jerked up on both my arms while trying to reach my face. The pillows got in the way, as I knew they would.

Duncan was off the bed in a nanosecond, ripping off the duct tape in one painful tear.

"You could have killed yourself," he said accusingly.

"Precisely."

"Stacey killed herself," said Martha, somewhat redundantly.

Duncan was looking disturbed.

"I didn't tamp the duct tape all the way down, Duncan. I could still breathe."

"Crazy little stunt," he said.

"With both of you guys there?"

"We might have fainted or something."

"She committed suicide." Martha was like a broken record.

"It's certainly another scenario," said Duncan as he balled up the duct tape and threw it in the trashcan.

"A woman diagnosed with Lou Gehrig's disease, with two years to live watching her body deteriorate around her," I said, and my mind went on a tangent thinking about Stacey and the demons she had faced.

"She had a motive for her own murder, no question," said Duncan. "But what's with the chloroform? Was she trying to say something? ... Cordi? Are you listening?"

I blankly looked at Duncan. The only thing I could say was, "All I've done is add another suspect to the list."

After that Martha and Duncan left and I spent some time looking through Martha's pictures. She was really very good, although there were no pictures of people, just animals. Some of the shots were out on the beach, some were in the forest, and, by the looks of it, some were just outside the door. My mind was whirling around so fast that I lost interest in the photos and went up to the mess to see who was around. Darcy and Trevor had taken the plywood off the windows. It was a beautiful day, so it wasn't surprising that no one was around. I went down to the labs to do some snooping and passed by an open door. It was a small office that might better be described as a closet. There were no windows and the lighting was dim. Every square inch was plastered with botanical plants of one sort or another.

"Cordi. What can I do for you?" I turned and saw Darcy bearing down on me.

"I was just wandering around."

"I see you've found my office," he said, a little too brightly.

"Sorry, didn't mean to pry."

He came up to me and nodded his head peremptorily.

On a whim I said, "Do you remember how Stacey was tied?"

He went pale then.

"So you do know?"

I took a guess at what he meant. "That it was suicide?"

He nodded, but I think it was because he was speechless.

"Was she depressed before she died?" I asked.

"Wouldn't you be?"

I took the deserved rebuff in stride and said, "I mean, did she behave any differently than she had over the previous five weeks?"

"She seemed resigned, if that's what you mean. She was never a happy person, but she did seem more depressed than usual. But then she became elated. That's the only word I can think of. As if she had made up her mind — I guess suicide was her only way out."

"But she was Catholic. That would have gone against her faith."

"It would have been against every moral fibre of her body to do it." His voice was shaking. "Her agony must have been intense. For her sake, I tried to stop you."

"Stop me?"

He looked disconcerted, as if he had said too much.

"Stop me from what?" I said and still he didn't answer. "Stacey's dead. What harm could it do for me to know?" I asked.

"A lot. That's my point. She would never want it known that she committed suicide. I had to keep you from finding out."

I looked at him with my jaw open. "You're the one who has been trying to kill me."

He cradled his forehead in his hand. "I was never trying to kill you, just scare you off the case. And it was just the lighthouse fire, nothing else."

"But what's the point? The police would have figured it out."

"Not without the primary clue."

"Which is?"

"That she was tied with slip knots. Only you and I knew that."

But I was momentarily distracted from Darcy as I remembered a conversation I had had and realized with a wallop that somebody else did know. I clued back in when he said, "With you out of the picture I just had to keep my mouth shut."

"But the ropes are physical evidence."

"Were physical evidence."

I looked at him with my mouth open. I could picture Stacey's raw wrists as we moved her up to the cooler, but there had been no ropes. He must have gone back to the crime scene before he asked me to address everybody.

I could hear someone on the phone down the hall and wondered if their conversation was going better than mine.

"You realize you have destroyed evidence that the police might need to charge someone with murder," I said.

"But I thought you agreed it was suicide," he said, his voice sharp and insistent.

"It could be, but it also could not be. The police will have to sort that one out. But for the record, you nearly succeeded in killing me. What were you thinking? Why did it matter so much to you?"

"She took a chance on me. I stole her laptop when I was her student at Dal. She caught me in the act and scared the shit out of me. Held me at gunpoint while she questioned every inch of my life. I must have answered the right way. In exchange for her silence she actually hired me as her assistant free of charge."

I must have looked surprised because Darcy chortled and said, "She pays me now."

I left Darcy and headed back to my cabin, thinking that Darcy could have killed Stacey to finally be free of her and the secret she carried.

Martha was snoring on her bed and had put all her photos and the printer on my bed. I really wanted to lie down but she was so peaceful looking that I picked up a handful of pictures and found a place to sit down at the end of my bed. I leafed through, looking at the pelicans skimming the sea, the male Indigo Bunting belting out its song of love, the feral pigs and the wild horses. I stopped at the picture of a screech owl. It was obviously taken at night but the little owl with the large ear tufts stood out. Its golden eyes stared at the camera, as if daring it to do something, which of course it had by taking the picture.

I was about to set the photo aside when something jumped out at me. I bent to look more closely. Behind the owl I could make out a cabin. But it wasn't the cabin that interested me. It was the person standing in the doorway and the time stamp on the image. My eyes weren't good enough to read it so I woke Martha up and she found the photo online. I was looking over her shoulder as she zeroed in on the face.

"What is Rosemary doing there?" said Martha. "I had no idea she was there when I took this picture."

"Do you remember where it was taken?"

"Yeah, that's right outside Stacey's cabin."

We digested what she had just said and then Martha zoomed in on the time stamp. July 22, 2:45 a.m.

"Isn't that around when Stacey died?" she asked.

"Zoom in on her left hand," and the left hand came into focus holding what looked like a roll of duct tape and some latex gloves. I had Martha zoom in on every section of the picture. We could see beyond Rosemary into the cabin and the back of Stacey's head slumped against the chair.

"Jesus. Did I capture the moment right after her death?" Martha quietly asked. "What are the odds?"

"Somehow I wouldn't have pegged Rosemary for a murderer," I said morosely. "I mean, she doesn't really have a motive."

"Cheer up, Cordi. Motive shmotive. We should be celebrating. You've solved the case."

But for some reason I didn't feel much like celebrating.

"Did you ever think that instead of murdering Stacey maybe she was helping her?" I said.

chapter twenty-five

I went looking for Darcy. In my haste I had forgotten I wanted to bring him up-to-date on everything so that someone would have all the facts to tell the police after I left the next morning. But after fifteen minutes of searching I couldn't find him.

I was at the bottom of the stairs to the mess when I heard a voice from above. I looked up and saw Mel. She was breathless.

"There's a snake," she said. "It's a copperhead. You told me you wanted to see one. It's at the lighthouse. If we go now it'll probably still be there. I spent the morning filming it."

We went on Mel's ATV and I found myself wishing I could stay on the island longer as we barrelled through the woods. By the time we got there I'd forgotten why we had come, so wrapped up was I in the stillness and beauty of the island. Mel led the way to the lighthouse and I wondered what the chances were that two snakes would climb those stairs to bask in the windows. We went up to the final turn in the stairs to the fourth window.

Mel was blocking my view when she suddenly said, "Damn. It's gone," which immediately made me look around in case I was about to step on it. And that's when I heard someone coming up the stairs, slowly, deliberately, and unhurried. I glanced at Mel but she was looking down the stairs. I called out but the steps kept coming. "Who's there?" I called out again. The steps stopped for a second and a voice came drifting up. "Rosemary." It sounded ghostly, echoey, creepy, and I had this weird premonition. I looked at Mel but she was still staring down the stairs as Rosemary came up out of the darkness.

She was different somehow — perhaps in the way she held herself, not mousy but strong and determined.

"The snake's out on the parapet basking in the sun." And she passed on by us on the way to the roof. Mel and I followed in silence. I was wondering if Rosemary had a special interest in snakes or was a clairvoyant when we all broke out onto the walkway that circled the top of the lighthouse. I could see the loose boards where I had almost fallen through. The view of the marching dunes, the swaying sea grass, the rolling waves, and the scudding clouds made me envy people who live by the sea. Its massive breadth and twisting, tumbling waves have got to be the closest thing to eternity that we have. That and the Himalayas. I brought my mind sharply back to the present.

"You think you're pretty smart, don't you?" Rosemary asked me as she manoeuvred herself between me and the lighthouse wall. I looked over the railing. It was still a long way down but this time there was no vine in the offing.

"I don't think I follow." But of course I did. I wondered how often somebody who helped somebody else commit suicide had ever been sentenced for the offence. Was that why Rosemary was acting the way she was? Or was it because she actually murdered Stacey in cold blood?

"You've spent the last three days snooping in other people's business."

"I'm sorry if that's a problem for you."

"Damn right it's a problem. You've found out too much for your own good."

"What, that you're a murderer?" I said with forced bravado.

Rosemary laughed. "Is that what you think? I thought you would have come up with a better theory than murder."

"How about suicide, then?"

She looked at me with some surprise and maybe a bit of respect.

"Suicide lets me off the hook," she finally said.

"Unless you helped her." I saw Mel flinch at that.

"Go on."

"Maybe Stacey decided to commit suicide but couldn't get up enough nerve to do it all on her own," I said.

"So I helped?"

"It's a scenario."

"Tell her it's not true," said Mel to Rosemary, her voice insistent.

I looked from Mel to Rosemary and back again. "You were in on it together."

Rosemary smiled and Mel frowned.

"How did you know I was thinking of suicide?" I asked.

Rosemary coughed and then said, "Mel. She overheard you talking with Darcy back at the station."

"But I really thought it was Wyatt," I said.

"Just what we wanted you all to think," said Rosemary.

I stared at her for several seconds and the penny dropped. "You were framing Wyatt with Stacey's suicide." It all finally came together. "You had her die for a murder conviction. You used her."

"You've got that last part wrong," said Rosemary. "Can't you see the beauty of it? It was our one way to get back at Wyatt for what he did to Stacey and to my sister, and we planned it together. I borrowed his clothes and stole his necklace and planted it all in Stacey's cabin, along with the boot and the cricket. I made everyone dislike him by making them believe he was beating me. That was really just overkill because no one much liked him anyway. He is a naturally nasty man. We even got him to handle the cheesecloth that we soaked in chloroform so that it would look like he knocked her out before tying her up. Stacey put it to her face to simulate that for the forensics guys."

"How did you know your sister and Stacey were victims of the same man?"

"The vet conference. I broke down and cried because my sister had only been dead a year and Wyatt had just been acquitted, the fucking bastard. Stacey lent me her shoulder to cry on." If Rosemary could have spit in anger she would have, her raw hatred exposed to the light. "So we hatched our plan and I took a job with him. He never knew who I was. I didn't attend the trial. Couldn't. It was too painful."

"You took a job with him. I'd hazard a guess that that would have been pretty painful too."

She stared at me. "It was the hardest thing I've ever done, being at his beck and call, always smiling, always helpful. But I knew where it was going so I was able to live with it."

"And Stacey?"

"Stacey saw me as a comrade in arms and Mel here as an innocent bystander, as were we all."

"Does Wyatt know who you really are?" I asked.

"Are you kidding? He'd kill me."

But I wasn't so sure. I remembered Wyatt asking for Rosemary's file. He must have had his suspicions.

"How did Wyatt know about Stacey and Mel?" I looked at Mel, whose eyes were as big and round as the harvest moon.

"He overheard a telephone conversation I had with Stacey months ago. I wasn't sure how much he had heard so I didn't tell Stacey. In hindsight it might have been a good idea to tell her."

"Stacey was afraid she'd lose her nerve and not be able to do it," said Mel. I glanced at Rosemary and saw a look of fear skitter across her face. Melanie continued. "She was a devout Catholic and it was against all she ever believed but this despicable excuse for a man made her turn her back on her faith."

"That and Lou Gehrig's disease," said Rosemary dryly. "And can you imagine having to carry to term a baby born of rape? What kind of agony, what kind of horrible sentence is that? She had a damn good reason to despise the man."

I glanced over at Melanie. She was crying and I wondered what kind of hell it would be to know you were born of rape. Which sentence was worse — the mother's or the daughter's?

"But Stacey changed her mind, didn't she?" I said and stared at Rosemary.

"Oh, no. She didn't," said Melanie, her words slightly garbled through the tears. "She was determined to nail Wyatt."

I looked at Rosemary. The fear was there again.

"You know too much, Cordi."

I looked down at the ground, so far, but just a five-second fall away, and shuddered.

And then I remembered. "The slip knots," I said.

"Exactly. You and Darcy and I are the only three who knew about them and Darcy destroyed the evidence. But I blew it. I referred to the slip knots when I was talking to you. I hoped you hadn't noticed. But it doesn't matter now. It's gone too far. You have become a liability."

Her eyes were so cold.

"You don't seem to be very good at killing me," I said, taking a stab at my own mortality.

She didn't move a muscle and her eyes didn't blink.

"Surely you didn't think I believed that Darcy would do more than just scare me? The flipped bike and a chase into the sea were beyond his abilities."

"So Darcy lit the fire." She laughed. "Too bad it didn't work."

"What are you saying, Rosemary?" said Mel, her voice ending on a very high note.

"Stay out of it, Mel."

"Stacey changed her mind, didn't she?" I repeated.

Rosemary tried to stare me down but then she smiled. "Yes." And in her decision to utter that one little word lay my death sentence.

"Nooooo!" wailed Mel.

"How did you know?" Rosemary ignored Mel and kept staring at me.

"A lucky guess, and the fact that her wrists were rubbed raw. She must have put up a big fight. A suicide would never have such marks unless they had a sudden change of heart."

"No, Rosemary. Tell her it's not true," Mel wailed.

Rosemary continued to ignore her. "I was the one who had to be with her in the end," said Rosemary. "I watched as she put the tape over her nose and mouth. We'd managed to get Wyatt's prints on the tape. It was my job to collect the gloves she wore."

"And to remove the roll of duct tape from the scene."

"No, that was sheer panic."

"You were running away from a woman begging for her life."

"Her eyes. They were awful. But we'd come so far. We finally had Wyatt. I couldn't let her change her mind."

"You goddamn bitch." Melanie screamed out the words and lunged at Rosemary.

I heard the boards splinter and watched helplessly as Rosemary and Mel fell over the edge. Frantically I reached out and grabbed Mel's hand, grabbing the railing with my other. The weight was agony. I tried to pull up but it was impossible.

"Help us," screamed Mel who had one hand on the edge of the parapet trying to support her weight and Rosemary's. "Rosemary's pulling my leg off. I can't hold on."

It seemed as though I was carrying them both and their dead weight was numbing. I was unable to do anything but hang on, and I knew I couldn't do that for very long.

"Her fingers are slipping. Get us up," cried Mel, but I couldn't budge and I could feel my grip slipping.

"She's got my shoe! It's slipping. It's slipping!"

I felt the weight lift and in that instant I let go of the rail, blocked out the sound of Rosemary screaming, and grabbed Mel's other hand. Before I could even think that I was nowhere near strong enough I reared back and hauled her over the edge. We landed in a pile on the splintered walkway and sat there in silence, gorging on air, our lungs hungry for it. Neither of us trusted the strength in our legs and it was some time before we went down to help Rosemary. But nothing could help Rosemary. She was gone.

We were in Mel's vehicle, heading back to the station, when I said to her, "What happened?"

"What do you mean?"

"You led me to believe you hated your mother's guts."

"I did. For most of my life." She fell silent.

"And?"

"And then I found out about Wyatt and what he had done to her." Her knuckles were white where she gripped the steering wheel.

"So why did you lie to me?"

"Because I couldn't tell you the truth."

"She must have loved you."

"How would you know?" she glanced at me.

"Because of the lock of hair in her locket."

"That was mine?" her voice went high and ended on a wail.

"Who else's could it have been?"

"I'm the child of a rapist," she said. "How could she love me?"

"Because she's your mother and there's nothing as strong as a mother's love." It sounded so trite, but it was true.

We drove along in silence for a while.

"Did your mother ask you to help frame Wyatt?" I asked.

"At first she didn't know that I knew Wyatt was my father, if that is what you mean. Rosemary said it was best that way and I agreed. It would have broken her heart."

"So Rosemary told you?"

"Yes. She thought I should know who my father was."

What would possess someone to tell someone else their father was a rapist? It was an unbelievably cruel thing to do and I marvelled at how blinded Rosemary had been to anything but her own situation.

"And she told Stacey that you knew."

"How could you know that?"

"She thought you should both know in the hopes that you would join her and your mother as an accomplice in the plot to frame Wyatt," I said.

"Why would she do that?" asked Melanie.

It was a rhetorical question, but I answered it anyway. "Because she knew your mother might have second thoughts, but I'm guessing she also knew how much Stacey loved you and that your influence could make the difference between going through with it or not."

"That's a pretty jaded view of things. My mother desperately wanted Wyatt put away forever. He'd ruined her life. More than anything she wanted to ruin his."

We were almost at the station when she blurted out, "Did you know that my mother once weighed a hundred and twenty pounds and was five feet nine inches tall? What he did to her made her hate herself and she ate and ate until she weighed more than three times what she had before. He dominated her life and she needed her revenge."

"And so did you. He tried to talk to you, didn't he?"

Her knuckles were white as she said, "Who told you?"

"I overheard him trying to get you to agree you were his daughter."

"The bastard. He couldn't leave well enough alone. He had to rub my face in his mess."

"Why did you do it? Why did you help your mother?"

"You have to ask?" she said and paused. "To see my mother get her revenge and escape a terrible death by ending her own life, with her daughter and her friend by her side."

"But you weren't by her side, were you?"

"No, I wasn't, I couldn't and I'll live with that for the rest of my life."

She started to cry as we came to a stop in the clearing. She got off the ATV and turned abruptly to leave, garbling about going to find Darcy to tell him about Rosemary. I offered to go with her but she was putting a brave face on things and wanted to go herself. I went back to my cabin, hoping Martha was there. She wasn't so I flopped on the bed and tried to relax but couldn't. I went up to the mess for a snack and to see who was about, but there was no one and I figured they must be out collecting Rosemary's body. When I went back out on the balcony Wyatt was there, gazing out over the clearing. He turned when he heard my footfall.

"Have you got your murderer?" he asked.

"You could say that," I said, not wanting to get into a conversation with him. But he wanted to talk and he was the type of guy who got what he wanted and I was too polite to ignore him.

"Three conniving little bitches, two down and one to go."

"I think the courts will look lightly on Mel," I said, between gritted teeth.

"She can't be allowed to get away with murder, can she? Even if she is my dear little daughter?"

"You did," I said. We stared at each other and I felt impotent, which made me angry.

"You killed Rosemary's sister."

"Case was thrown out," he said with a supercilious smile on his face.

"Through lack of evidence, not through lack of guilt," I retorted.

He smiled again and I had this overwhelming urge to wipe it off his face.

"You don't really give a damn about your daughter, do you?"

"Oh goody goody, here comes the rap-me-on-the-knuckles speech."

"You should be in jail. You raped Stacey and murdered Rosemary's sister."

"Did I hear you say, 'among others'?" He smiled then and I shuddered. There'd been others?

"I am completely innocent in Stacey's death."

"How can you say that? You raped her and left a daughter to be raised in foster homes. You destroyed their lives."

"You mean had consensual sex with, don't you?" he said with a leer. "Anyway, that's Stacey's fault. She should have looked after our daughter better."

"Do you have any idea what it must have been like for her? To have to have a child born of rape."

"She could have had an abortion."

"She was Catholic. Her parents were Catholic. She had no choice."

"Bullshit. What's the big deal anyway? You get knocked up. You either abort or have it. She just liked the attention. The way I see it I did her a favour." He laughed. "I gave her a purpose in life."

"You're going to jail for a very long time." I said it without thinking, biting my anger back.

He looked momentarily disconcerted but then the old smirk was back. "And just how do you intend to do that? Are you going to fight my cases the way you did your other murders up in Quebec and in the Arctic? With clumsy good luck?"

"No," I said as evenly as I could. Clumsy good luck! I could have killed him. "Nothing as mundane as that. The police have new evidence that has come to light in Rosemary's sister's case. They are going to reopen it."

I stared him down, knowing that I'm not a very good liar but really believing that I could find that evidence, and needing him to believe it too.

"That new evidence is irrefutable and will nail you securely to the maximum-security-prison wall. You're going down for multiple lifetimes."

And there it was. The smirk was gone. He went very pale and his eyes darted about as if they'd lost their anchor.

He moved over toward the railing like an automaton and too late I realized I had never put up the orange tape. I hesitated and in that moment of hesitation he leaned against the railing. It splintered and pulled away from the verandah and Wyatt went with it.

For the next couple of hours things were pretty chaotic, with two more bodies joining Stacey in the cooler. Darcy insisted on putting Melanie under house arrest until the police came, and everybody was talking about what drove Stacey and Rosemary and Melanie to do what they did. Revenge is an evil thing. It takes hold like a cancer, growing and growing and spreading and spreading until its only outlet is action. Lives ruined at the hand of a sick man who never paid for his crimes. And his influence still stalked its prey, still stalked Mel, still stalked me. The way he died had me second-guessing myself a million times and I could see him laughing at that.

He died because of me.

He died because I didn't like him.

He died because I hesitated.

And I find I am glad that I did. And that is what haunts me the most.

acknowledgements

Thank you to my good friend Rebecca Bell, who, besides making excellent comments on *Dying for Murder*, taught me a great deal about barrier islands and sea turtles, and made sure I never ate pork chops ten nights in a row again. Thanks also to Jim Richardson and Nicholas Mrosovsky who introduced me to barrier islands and sea turtles. Thanks to ma soeur, Dorion Kingsmill, and my sons, Tim Kingsmill Wootton and Jesse Kingsmill Wootton, for reading over various drafts and providing excellent comments and suggestions. Thanks for the many lunchtime conversations at Pho Vietnam! Thanks to Age of the Geek, where I finished writing the book, between important lunches and coffee breaks. Thanks also to Sandy Macdonald for my author photo on the Dundurn website and for his voice on my book trailer (www.youtube.com/watch?v=YLXKIF36Su0) and so much more. And thanks to Kirk Howard and the team at Dundurn. You rock!

From the Same Series

Forever Dead
A Cordi O'Callaghan Mystery
Suzanne F. Kingsmill
978-1-550027051
$11.99

The discovery of a bear-ravaged body abandoned in the wilderness, some killer rapids, a fumigated lab, stolen research disks, and a stalled career all coalesce into the ripening madness that hauls zoology professor Cordi O'Callaghan into some very wild, very dangerous places.

While the police label the wilderness mauling an accidental death, Cordi realizes that the theft of her disks is somehow related to the body found in the woods. She must unsnarl the mess if she is to salvage her academic career. Cordi's athletically ingenious and hair-raising solutions to deadly encounters keep her one stumble ahead of a murderer as she follows a path littered with motives. But nothing can prepare her for the final shocking twist that leaves her with a wrenching dilemma — one that no one with a conscience should have to face.

Innocent Murderer

A Cordi O'Callaghan Mystery

Suzanne F. Kingsmill

978-1-554884261

$11.99

When zoology professor Cordi O'Callaghan reluctantly accepts an invitation to be a lecturer aboard the *Susanna Moodie*, a vessel ferrying tourists through Canada's Arctic, she figures it will be a breeze. Seasickness aside, Cordi becomes entangled in the deaths of two of her fellow passengers, both members of a close-knit fiction-writing group. The fatalities are ruled accidental, but Cordi suspects they're anything but. However, she lacks evidence and credibility, according to Martha Bathgate and Duncan Mcpherson, her sometimes reluctant sidekicks who try to keep her grounded.

After Cordi returns to her home in the Ottawa Valley, she hits the trail and stirs up a hornet's nest of lies, intrigue, jealousy, and greed as she grills potential murderers, one of whom takes offence and stalks her. Getting marooned on pack ice, a harrowing trip in an airplane and a hot air balloon, and a mysterious fire all add to the menace that threatens Cordi as she attempts to nail down a killer.

Available at your favourite bookseller

 **DUNDURN**

Visit us at

Dundurn.com | @dundurnpress

Facebook.com/dundurnpress | Pinterest.com/dundurnpress